Southern Chance

SPECIAL EDITION

NATASHA MADISON

Copyright

One

KALLIE
EIGHT YEARS AGO

"Senior prom!" I exclaim, looking over at Jacob in his suit with the white rose pinned on his jacket lapel. We just left my house where we must have taken a million pictures. "Can you believe it? In just a few more months, we will both be in our own little apartment off campus." I smile over at him, and even in the dark, I see his blue eyes shining at me. Leaning over, I kiss him and can still taste the punch on his lips.

Jacob and I have been two peas in a pod for as long as I can remember. Every memory, good or bad, was always with Jacob by my side. It also helped that our moms met one day at the local coffee shop and became best friends. We had sleepovers way before we knew what sleepovers were. He was my best friend, and if I'm going to be honest, I fell in love with him when I was seven and he carried me inside after scraping my knees. I never looked at him in any other way until grade seven when he started dating Becky Statson, and I suddenly went from liking her to loathing everything about her.

The old saying "you don't know what you have until someone else has it" is one hundred percent the truth. I waited

1

with bated breath while they dated. When they finally broke up, I confessed my feelings for him, and we've been a couple ever since. He was my first kiss, my first everything, and I knew that it would only be a matter of time until we got married. Growing up in a small town meant everyone expected us to get married right out of high school, so even our parents were surprised with our decision not to get married right away.

We pull up to the school, and he parks in his regular parking spot. The music from inside seeps out, and the disco ball and lights can be seen flashing in the windows. People go in and out, and some hang around outside. Jacob gets out of the car and walks over to my side, opening my door. His hand reaches out to help me, and then he closes the door. I thought he did this to be romantic, but he told me he did this so he can pin me to the side of the car and make out with me. I did not care in the least. "You're going to crush your flower," I say right before he pushes me into the side of his truck and his lips meet mine. "It's a stupid flower anyway." My hands go around his neck, and just like all the other times he kisses me, he leaves me smiling and my stomach fluttering. "You owe me a dance, Mr. McIntyre."

"Well, Miss Barnes, let's go, so I can give you your dance and then we can go, and I can show you my surprise." He grabs my hand and walks away from the truck and toward the school.

"I've seen that surprise already." I look at him and laugh. "It's a nice surprise. It's just after the first fifty times, it's not really a surprise anymore." He just shakes his head, and we are about to walk up the steps when we hear someone call Jacob's name. I turn to see Savannah wearing her regular clothes. She looks sad, like she's been crying, and I'm suddenly concerned for her.

Savannah, Jacob, and Beau have been best friends since birth almost. Savannah's mom worked for Beau's mother as their housekeeper. Beau and Jacob just grew up in the same circle since Jacob's father was the sheriff, and Beau's father was the mayor.

"Hey." I smile at her. We are friends, but it's only through Jacob.

"Hey," Savannah says, and she walks closer to us. She is the most beautiful girl I've ever seen. With long legs and perfect hair, you would think she was a model. "I was wondering if I could talk to Jacob." She looks at me, and I look at Jacob. I know he always protects her, and the bond they have is more sister and older brother than anything else.

"I'm going to head in," I say. "Come and find me." I kiss his lips, and he just smiles at me. Walking up the steps, I head into the school and down the hallway toward the gym where the party is at. I see a couple of people I know and stop to talk to them. I enter the gym with the music blaring, and balloons are everywhere. The overhead lights are off, but the DJ has some lights flashing from white to blue to red. I wave to a couple of people and then finally find my friends, who greet me with hugs. We take pictures and joke and laugh. I really don't know how long I'm in the gym when the whispers start.

"I think she's pregnant," one girl whispers, and I look around and try not to feel like they are looking at me.

"You think she knows?" another one says, holding her glass of punch and taking a sip, trying not to stare at me. My neck suddenly gets warm and dread fills me, but I have no idea why. I look around and see eyes focused on me but they dart away once I look at them. Making my way through the people in the gym, I walk down the hallway again back outside, and I see Jacob and Savannah over to the side talking near a tree. Their conversation seems heated, and my feet feel like they are stuck in concrete blocks. No matter how fast I want to run to him, they seem to be going farther and farther away.

Walking down the steps, I spot Beau walking up the steps.

He's wearing a blue suit with a white shirt and a blue bow tie. His black hair is perfectly cut and coiffed to the side. His blue eyes almost look black with the darkness around us. "You clean up nice." He smiles at me, and his whole face lights up. I roll my eyes and pick up my dress so he can see my worn cowboy boots that I'm trying to hide.

"You can take the girl out of the country, but you can't ..." Beau starts saying, almost laughing.

"Take the boots off her feet." I finish the sentence for him and push his shoulder jokingly.

"Where is the mister?" he asks, and I point at the tree where Savannah and Jacob are. Something about their conversation makes me feel uneasy. I walk past Beau and make my way over to them.

"You can't seriously be saying this," Savannah says in a tone that makes me want to get there faster. "I can't."

"Hey," I say when I finally get close enough to them to see that Savannah is crying. "Is everything okay?" I look at her, and then I look at Jacob, who avoids looking at me. "What's going on?" I ask. My stomach suddenly falls, and I don't know why. It's like my body knows something bad is coming and is preparing itself, but my brain doesn't know. Neither say anything, nor do they make eye contact with me. My hands start to get clammy, and my heart feels like it's beating out of my chest. "Jacob." I say his name, and he looks up at me with tears in his eyes.

"I'm so sorry," he says. I don't know if I understand what's going on. "Kallie." He takes a step closer to me, but my instinct is to take a step back. "I can explain."

My mouth gets dry, and the lump in my throat makes it hard for me to swallow. "Someone better say something and something fast," Beau says when he sees me start to shake, coming over to me and holding me around my shoulders. He shouldn't be the one holding me, it should be Jacob.

"Say it." The words come out softly as my head starts to spin, and I try to wake myself up from this bad dream. This has to be a bad dream. This can't be happening, not to me.

"She's pregnant." He repeats the words I heard whispered in the gym. I wait for him to continue, wait for him to tell me that what I'm thinking isn't true. I wait for him to tell me anything. This is Jacob. He wouldn't do this to me. He wouldn't hurt me like this, not the Jacob who holds me during scary movies and brings me ice cream when I'm not in a good mood. Not my Jacob. "I'm so sorry."

"Oh my God." My knees buckle, and Beau's hold on me tightens to make sure I don't hit the ground. But he can't stop the roiling of my stomach, and I put my hand to my mouth to keep from being sick, but it doesn't help. I get sick right here in front of them. Jacob tries to take a step to me, the tears now streaming down his face. "No!" I shout at him, holding up my hand to stop him from approaching me. Beau squats down beside me and hands me a handkerchief from his pocket. Grabbing the linen handkerchief, I hold it over my mouth.

"Kallie, let me take you somewhere, and I can explain," he says, but I just shake my head, not listening to the words, and then I look at her. The woman who I accepted as a friend, the woman who I never expected would do what she just did. The woman who has taken away everything that I thought I knew.

"How could you?" I ask, and she just sobs in front of me, holding her hands folded in front of her.

"It's not what you think," she says, and I laugh bitterly, but the sob rips through me.

"You're wrong," I say. "It's worse than I think." I then look at Beau. "Can you take me home?"

"Kallie." Jacob steps forward again and puts his hand on my arm, the same hand that just held my hand, the hand that made my stomach flutter every single time he touched me.

Except this time, it's like he's burning my skin, so I jerk my arm away from his touch. "Please let me explain."

"You slept with her while you told me you loved me!" I shout at him, the tears leaking out of my eyes faster than I can wipe them away. I don't even notice the crowd forming around us. "You slept with her while you made plans with me about the future. Our future." My voice grows even louder.

"Kallie." Beau says my name softly, and I look at him.

"You knew." Pointing at him, I say, "You had to have known. You guys are the three musketeers."

"No," he says, shaking his head. "I didn't know."

"I don't believe you," I say, and then I look back at Jacob. "I hope she's worth it." I turn and make my way through the crowd. Out of nowhere, my brother's truck turns the corner of the school parking lot, and he pulls up to the curb right where I am. I don't know how he knew, but when he stops at the curb, I open the truck door. "How did you ...?"

"Beau," he says, and I nod my head while he drives off with the sound of Jacob shouting my name in the background. "He can't find me," I say to him, and he just nods. I lean my head on the truck door, closing my eyes and letting the memories of Jacob fade away.

Two

KALLIE
EIGHT YEARS LATER

"How much longer?" I look over at my best friend, Olivia, and then turn my focus on the dark road ahead of me. We've been on the road for over fourteen hours, only stopping to get gas and go to the bathroom while we grab some food.

"We are going to have to pull over," I say. "I can barely keep my eyes open, and we still have twelve hours to go." She takes her phone out of the center cup holder and unlocks it.

"There is a motel six minutes from here," she says, "but I'm not sure they are even open. The last reviews are from two years ago."

"What about a chain hotel?" I ask.

"There is a Hilton twenty-five minutes from here." She swipes her phone and then looks at me. "It's reserved."

"Did you use your credit card?" I ask, tapping my fingers on the steering wheel. The last thing I expected yesterday when I woke up was that my life would spiral out of control and I would be heading to the one place I ran from.

"I used one of the credit cards we bought." She holds up

the MasterCard gift card we purchased right before hightailing it.

I look over at her and think back to four years ago when we started working for the same magazine, just in different departments. One day, we had to work together on a project, and we just clicked. From that day, we became almost inseparable. She pretends to smile, but it doesn't work.

"Fine, we can get some pizza," I say and walk to the reception area. I give my name at the check-in desk and get the key card for our room. We walk to the elevator and take it up to the third floor.

"Fine, I'll take it," she says, and we get out of the elevator and then walk down the well-worn brown carpet. "This is not a four-star," she mumbles next to me. I want to tell her that it is, but the peeling wallpaper will not help my case.

I insert the card into the reader, and the door unlocks when the light shines green. The smell of stale air fills the room, but when I flip on the light, it's not as bad as I think we both expected it to be. The two double beds have white blankets on them. I step in, and the bathroom door is to the left. I flip on the light and see that the bathtub is a faded yellow color, and the white shower curtain has seen better days. "I call dibs," Olivia mumbles as the door slams behind her. She kicks off her sneakers, then slides off her purse and dumps it on the small wooden desk in the corner.

She sits on the bed, and I watch her put her face in her hands. "I hate him." Looking up at me, she has tears running down her face. "How could he do this to me, to all those people?"

"I don't know." I shake my head. "Do you want some wine?" Looking around the room, I wonder if there is a minibar in the hotel room. I spot the fridge in the corner underneath the television stand, and when I open it, the horrible smell makes me gag. "Well, that would be a no," I say, holding my hand up to my nose to smell my shirt.

"The universe hates me." Olivia gets up from the bed. "I'm going to take a bath." She starts walking to the bathroom. "Or maybe not. I have no idea."

"You go wash," I say, "and I'm going to get the lay of the land."

"Your Southern accent is coming out." Olivia chuckles. "It took you two years to stop saying y'all."

Shaking my head, I grab the key card I had thrown on the desk and walk out into the hallway. Taking the elevator down to the lobby, I ask the receptionist who checked us in if there is someplace close to buy wine.

"Not at this time of night," she says. I glance down at my phone and see it's nine p.m. We are definitely not in New York City anymore.

"Is there anywhere we can get something to eat?" I ask, looking around for any menus that might be lingering around.

"No, the Piggly Wiggly closes at eight during the week." She smiles at me, and I shake my head.

"I assume you have vending machines somewhere?" I ask, looking around, and her eyes go big.

"Yes." She walks around the desk to a room in the corner. "Here are the machines." She points at two vending machines. One is filled with chips and chocolates, and the other has soft drinks.

"I think I'm going to need change," I say, seeing that everything is seventy-five cents.

"No worries. If you want, I can open the machine for you and just hand you what you want." She smiles at me, walking out of the room to get the key to open the machine.

By the time I get back into the room, the shower is still running. I dump the ten packs of chips, chocolate bars, Oreo cookies, Cheez-It snacks, some peanuts, and a honey bun on the side table in the middle of the two beds. The water shuts off as soon as I kick off my shoes, and my phone rings. I pick it up and see it's Casey.

"Hey." I answer the phone softly.

"Hey, yourself," he says, and I hear the covers rustle in the background. "Where are you?"

"No clue," I say, sitting on the bed and falling back. "Someplace that has a Piggly Wiggly." He laughs.

"That could be anywhere from Alabama to Florida."

"I think we have another twelve hours to go," I say. "Why was it a good idea to drive?"

"Because your flight can be traced here, and if your friend wants to stay under the radar, the best thing to do is drive," he says, and I shake my head. "Either way, I'm happy you're finally coming home."

"Don't start with me, Casey," I say. "I get enough of a guilt trip from Mom when I don't come home for the holidays."

"Yeah, well, she's already cleaning out your old room and cooking all your favorite dishes." He laughs. "Expect lots of home-cooked meals," he whispers, "with butter."

"God," I groan. "I just got under one hundred and ten pounds. Do you know how many hot yoga sessions I had to do and salads I had to eat? Kale is not tasty."

"It is if it's deep fried and then drenched in butter," he says. "Anyway, I'm off to bed. Five a.m. comes quickly."

"I'll be home tomorrow. I am going to push through," I say. The bathroom door opens, and Olivia comes out in a cloud of steam. "See you then," I say and disconnect.

Olivia has her hair wrapped up in a white towel and another towel wrapped around her chest, and she's carrying her clothes in a ball in her hand. "That shower felt great." She dumps her clothes on the bed and comes over to the food that I bought. "What do we have here?"

"The second-best thing I could get," I say, getting up to a sitting position. "The Piggly Wiggly is closed."

"I don't know if I should be happy about that or sad," she says, grabbing the trail mix and opening it. "Maybe sad." She turns and walks back to the bathroom to spit it out. "That trail mix is at least a year old."

"I have no doubt the chips are fresh," I say. Getting up, I walk over to the bathroom and turn on the water. "I want to be gone by three if that's okay."

"Yeah," Olivia says, sitting on the bed with four bags of chips and two Snickers. "Why did we stop eating chips?" she asks after shoving five into her mouth.

"I mean, it's a carb," I say, pulling off my sweater, "and deep fried, and there is a fuck ton of sodium."

"I don't care," she says, putting another handful into her mouth and opening the Snickers. "God, I forgot how much I love chocolate," she says, taking another bite.

I shake my head and take a fast shower, letting the heat hit my neck. I won't admit it, but I'm nervous as fuck about going back home. I said I would never go back there, and now here I am, twelve hours away from driving back into a town I never wanted to return to.

When I get out of the shower, I wrap myself the same way that Olivia did, and when I walk out, she's under the covers and the wrappers from two chocolate bars are on the side table with a bag of chips. "I remember now why we stopped," she groans. "I feel sick."

"That's because your body isn't used to sugar or starch," I say, laughing. Getting a shirt, I put it on with my underwear. I pick up my phone and set the alarm for two forty-five. "What are the chances that we'll hit a Starbucks tomorrow morning?"

I slip under the cold white covers and turn off the light. "I'm going to say almost zero, but you never know." I put my head down on the pillow.

"Thank you," she says, and I look over at her in the dark room, "for going back home. I know that the last thing you want to do is go back there."

"It'll be fine," I say, ignoring the hammering of my heart. "I'm just not sure you're ready for it."

"I'm ready," she says softly, and I close my eyes, falling asleep within minutes. When the alarm goes off, I groan, reaching over and seeing that Olivia is sitting up in bed.

"Did you sleep?" I ask, blinking away the sleep.

"For an hour, I think." Her voice is soft. "I gave up after I had a nightmare." Ever since she was arrested, she wakes up with nightmares.

"I'm ready," she says, tossing off her covers to show me she's dressed in jeans and a tank top.

"I'll be ready in five," I say, getting up and walking to the bathroom. I pee in the dark and get dressed, not even turning on the light when I brush my teeth. When I walk out of the bathroom, the lights are on, and she's sitting on the bed eating another bag of chips. She has a sweater on now and her Gucci flops. I don't tell her that she's going to have to put running shoes on once we get to the farm. Instead, I grab my bag.

"I have the rest of the food," Olivia says, getting up and walking to the door. I'm not a morning person and never have been. I need at least two cups of coffee, and that's before I can even see straight. We walk past the unoccupied reception desk and outside into the cold air.

"It'll heat by nine," I say, unlocking the car door and getting in. We don't hit a Starbucks, but we do find a coffee shop. I order three cups of coffee, finishing one as soon as we sit back in the car. We pick up a couple of sandwiches, and the closer I get to home, the more my nerves kick into gear.

"It's going to be fine." I give myself a pep talk when I look over at Olivia, who's asleep in the passenger seat.

Getting off at the exit, I slowly make my way down Main

Street, trying not to look around or even slow down. Instead, I focus on heading to my family's farm. "I swear it looks just like a Hallmark movie," Olivia says while she looks outside in awe, and I want to groan. "Fuck," she says, and then I make the mistake of looking out the window when we come to a stop sign. I look over to see black hair.

He walks down the two steps of the sheriff's office, but I would know that walk anywhere. When I left eight years ago, he was just a boy, and now he is all man. No matter what I tell myself or say out loud, just looking at him makes my heart ache even more than it did before. His chest is bigger, his arms are thicker, and his five o'clock is shadow setting in.

I watch him walk, looking down, and then turn around to see a boy come running toward him. He smiles at him and bends down to catch the boy with blond hair. He picks him up in his arms and buries his face in his neck. I was wrong before, the pain of leaving him was nothing compared to the pain I feel now as I watch him with his son.

I don't even know how long I'm at the stop sign, but a honking horn makes everyone look at my car, and the smile that was on his face a couple of seconds ago is gone, and in its place is a glare as he watches me drive away for a second time.

Three

JACOB

"How many days are you off now?" I look up from my desk and see Monica standing there with her arms crossed over her chest. She's been with me since I took over the sheriff's office after my father died suddenly four years ago. I was already the second in command at that point, so it was a no-brainer I would take over for him.

My eyes roam up and down as she stands there in a tight black skirt and white silk shirt. She is way overdressed for working in the office, and she doesn't even hide the fact that she wants to be under me. "I don't know what I'm going to do without seeing you." She twirls her bleached blond hair around her finger.

I lean back in the chair, the squeak coming out of the wooden chair that once belonged to my father. "I'm sure you'll be fine." I smile at her. "Besides, I think that Grady is on all weekend." Grady is my second in command. We graduated from the academy together and started on the same day. He's had a hard-on for Monica since the day she sauntered in here.

"I have a couple of things to do before I head out," she says, turning around and walking away. My eyes go straight to her ass. Fuck, I need to get laid. Looking down at my hands, the right and the left, I wonder which one is going to get lucky tonight.

The phone on my desk beeps, and I look down and see that it's Casey.

Casey: *We need to talk.*

I toss my phone down, not even interested in what he has to say. My relationship with him ended the day he took Kallie away from me. My hands clench into fists just thinking about her. The woman who I used to love with everything I had, but now I hate more than anyone in the world. My phone beeps again, and it's him again.

Casey: *I'm not fucking around with you.*

I shake my head and answer him back.

Jacob: *I don't want or need to hear what you have to say.*

I press send while another text comes in from Beau.

Beau: *What time is the game tonight?*

I answer him right away.

Jacob: *Six p.m. is kickoff.*

Beau: *See you there.*

I run my hands over my face, my back protesting the movement. I have the next four days off, and I plan to sleep all day long. When my phone beeps again, I groan.

Savannah: *Hey, I got called in to the bar. Can I drop Ethan off early?*

Jacob: *I'm at the station.*

Savannah: *Be right there.*

I put my phone on the desk and look over at the picture of me and my son. His smile is everything. He is everything. My mind goes to a place I never let it go.

On prom night eight years ago, Kallie sat next to me, looking more beautiful than ever. With her face done up in light makeup and her long blond hair curled at the bottom, I couldn't

15

wait to take her back to the barn where I had a special surprise for her. The little black box in my suit jacket pocket suddenly felt heavy. From as far back as I could remember, there wasn't a memory that I had—good or bad—that didn't have Kallie in it. But when she finally admitted that she loved me, everything just came together. I loved her. She was everything to me.

We got to the school, and I wanted to leave, but I had promised her a dance. I didn't even see Savannah when we pulled up, but she stepped out of the shadows, and I saw right away that she was crying.

Savannah, Beau, and I had always had a special bond. Beau as my best friend and Savannah as the pain in the butt who never left our side. She was always the kid picked on because her mother was the help. She would get hand-me-downs and be known as "a boy" since she always dressed in hand-me-downs that either Beau or Liam wore. Beau and I were always saving her one way or another.

"What's wrong?" I asked her right away, looking around to see if someone was around her.

"I'm in trouble," she said, her voice shaking. "So much trouble."

"What do you mean?" I asked her while people walked around us all dressed up.

"I don't know how it happened," she said and then sobbed, and I took her in my arms.

"It's going to be okay." I rubbed her hair. "Whatever it is, it's going to be okay."

"I'm pregnant," she said, and I let go of her, stepping back.

"Oh my God." My hand flew to my mouth. "Who?"

"I ..." She looked down at the ground and sobbed out again. "I can't tell you that."

"What are you going to do?" I asked her as I ran my hand through my hair. This was crazy because she was already looked down at all the time.

"I know that you and Kallie are going away, but if you can just ..." she said at the same time I started to shake my head.

"You can't be serious." I gasped out at her. "I can't. Think about this for a second, Savannah. You have to tell the father." I tried to reason with her.

"I can't." She shook her head and put her hand on her stomach.

"Then you have to think about maybe adoption." I tried to make her see, but it just got her even more hysterical. I was almost at my wits' end. "What about perhaps ..." I didn't want to say the words, but she read between the lines.

"You can't seriously be saying this," Savannah hissed. "I can't."

"Hey." I heard Kallie's voice from behind me, and I knew it was going to just blow up. "Is everything okay?" she asked, looking first at Savannah and then at me, and my eyes avoided hers. I couldn't look at her. "What's going on?" Her voice was frantic at one point, and she called my name. "Jacob." I knew then and there my life would change. I just didn't know if I would survive it.

"I'm so sorry," I said, and it was as if she knew that her life would be changed also. Her body started to shake, and I called her name. "Kallie." I took a step forward, but she just took a step backward away from me. "I can explain."

I watched her eyes go blank. I watched her shut down in front of me, and then I heard Beau shouting. I looked at him, and for one second, I wished he got here first. That he was the one who Savannah went to. "Someone had better say something and something fast." He wrapped his arm around Kallie as she started to shake.

"Say it." She looked at me, so broken, so helpless. It was like I was looking in a mirror.

"She's pregnant." I said the words that would forever change the path of my life. She looked at me, waiting for me to tell her

17

that it wasn't mine and assure her that I would never do that to her. I thought she would know. I thought she would have had enough faith in me and our love to automatically know that wasn't true. I prayed that she saw what was in my eyes. That I loved her all the way down to my soul. "I'm so sorry."

"Oh my God," she said, her knees buckling under her, and she got sick on the sidewalk. The tears rushed out of me as my heart broke and my chest got tight, so tight I didn't think I would be able to breathe.

"Kallie. Please, baby," I pleaded with her while she looked up and shouted.

"No!" Her hand shot up and blocked me from her.

"Kallie, let me take you somewhere, and I can explain." I almost got on my knees and begged her, and all she could do was look at Savannah, who stood there crying.

"How could you?" Kallie asked Savannah with hatred in her voice, and she had every reason to.

"It's not what you think," Savannah tried to tell her, but the sob ripped right through her.

"You're wrong." She stood up and tried to hold her shoulders high. My brave, brave girl. "It's worse than I think." She ignored me and looked at Beau. "Can you take me home?"

"Kallie." I stepped forward to put my hand on her, and she ripped her arm away from my touch, so I let my hand fall to my side. "Please let me explain." I wanted to rip my hair out. I wanted to shout the truth and tell her that it wasn't true. Nothing about this was true.

"You slept with her while you told me you loved me!" she shouted at me, each word like a knife to my heart as tears poured down both of our cheeks. Every dream I'd ever had of us getting married and having children together was erased, like it never was. "You slept with her while you made plans with me about the future. Our future." Her voice was so loud that I finally spotted a crowd around us. The pain ripped through me, gutting me,

leaving me hollow. I just had to get her alone so I could explain it to her.

"Kallie." Beau said her name, and she turned her anger on him also.

"You knew." Kallie pointed at him. "You had to have known. You guys are the three musketeers."

"No," he said, shaking his head. He looked as gutted as Kallie looked right now. "I didn't know."

"I don't believe you," she hissed, and then she looked at me. "I hope she's worth it." She turned and walked through the crowd, and my eyes followed her, my feet stuck to the ground. As I looked around, the crowd just looked at me. Some with disgust and others with sorrow.

She got into Casey's truck, and he peeled off. She was leaving me, and I ran, I ran so fast after the truck. I pushed myself, calling her name over and over until my voice was raw. I ran until my legs burned and my knees buckled, leaving me in the middle of the road with the sight of the red taillights fading.

The phone rings, bringing me back to the present. My chest hurts just as bad as it did that day, just the same as it has since she left. "Hello?"

"You're a hard man to get a hold of," Casey says, and I roll my eyes.

"Not a hard man to get a hold of. Me not answering you should have been a clue that I have nothing to say to you."

"Listen, I don't have much time," he says with attitude, and I laugh.

"Actually, me neither," I say, and I hang up on him. Fuck him, he kept me from her. The next day, he kicked me off his property and refused to let me see Kallie. Then two days later, her father told me she was gone, and I found out he snuck her out of town.

Grabbing my keys, I say goodbye to Monica while I walk out into the hot Southern heat. I'm walking down the steps when I hear Ethan call my name. "Dad!" he shouts, and I turn to look at him. Luckily for both of us, my son looks exactly like Savannah, but he's my son right down to my bones. I bend to catch him while he runs to me, and I bury my face into his neck, giving him a kiss. His laughter gets louder, and then I hear cars honking. I look at where it's coming from, and it's like I'm brought back to eight years ago. It has to be because there is no way I am actually seeing what I am seeing.

Kallie, looking as beautiful as she did when she walked away from me without giving me a second thought. The same Kallie who said she would always stand by me. The same Kallie I slowly started to hate. "Oh my God." I look at Savannah beside me. "Is that Kallie?" she asks.

Four

KALLIE

"Oh my God, oh my God, oh my God." I keep chanting it over and over again, and I blink away the tears that have formed in my eyes the minute I saw him with his son. His son.

"Kallie," Olivia whispers. She puts her hand on mine, and I just shake my head. "Is that him?"

"Oh, that was him all right." I wipe away the lone tear that escapes and rolls down my cheek. "He and his son and probably his wife."

"Probably his wife?" she asks. "Probably?"

My hands grip the steering wheel so hard my knuckles are white. "I don't exactly know."

"And why don't you know?" She throws her hands up and huffs.

"Because I didn't want to know," I say, turning onto the gravel road that leads to my family's property. "After I left, I didn't want to know."

"But how?" She looks out the window as the trees pass us by.

"They tried to, but I shut it down. I told them I would no

longer call if they even brought him up." I take a deep inhale. "I couldn't think of him with her, and I didn't want to know. I locked it away and refused to even think about it."

"How is this going to work now that we are in town?" I've been asking myself that same question since we started our drive. It would be easy to pretend he didn't exist. But now that I was home and he was so close, I knew my heart wouldn't be able to withstand it, and I was not wrong. The pain of losing him is even more now than before. The ache in my chest is a combination of pressure and little stabs of pain.

"I'm going to make it work," I say, trying not to make her feel any worse than she already does about bringing me back home. "Besides, I think it's a big enough town that I won't run into him."

"Dude, we've been in your town for a hot minute, and you've run smack into him." Olivia points in the direction where we can from. "Literally one street."

"I know that, Olivia," I say harshly. "I get it, but right now, I can't fall apart, okay? I'm going to see my parents, and the last thing they need to see is me being a fucking basket case." I blink as fast as I can, ignoring the stinging in my eyes. "It took a month for them to get me up and out of bed when I left here."

"It'll be okay," she says softly. "Everything is going to be okay, and if it's not, we can leave and go back home." We drive into a clearing, and you can finally see my property. There are four black stallions running free in the fence enclosure on the right side.

"Oh, wow," Olivia says, her eyes looking around at the vast green that surrounds my parents' huge house. "You lived here?" she asks, gesturing to the huge white farmhouse where my mom and father still live. The same house where my mother grew up. The sight of the house makes my heart speed up just a touch, and when I finally turn into the parking area beside the house, all I can hear is the gravel crunching under the car. The sound is suddenly louder than I ever remembered.

I look over at the house. "They painted the house," I say. The fresh white paint was applied not too long ago since it still shines. My mother opens the front screen door, and she walks out onto the covered porch, waving excitedly at us. I turn the car off and look over at Olivia. "Here goes nothing."

Opening the car door, I put one foot out of the car before the smell of the horses hits me. It really is country. I smile to myself, and the sudden memories of me riding the horses come back to me in full force; the memories of falling off them, and the ones of me and Jacob going on the secret trails we found. It's all too much, and I want to run away again. I want to hightail it out of here just like I did eight years ago.

"Kallie," my mother says. She rushes down the two steps and hurries over the little concrete path in front of the house. I look at her, and she looks just the same as she did four years ago when she flew out to see me. Her hair is a touch whiter, but she is still in her jeans and a T-shirt. I turn and walk around the car and rush to her. She holds her arms out, and the minute I smell her, I fall apart in her arms. "It's okay, sweetheart," she says softly, smoothing my hair. "It's going to be okay."

"Mom." I just say her name as I hug her harder than I ever have in my whole life. I've missed her so much. I didn't know how much until I hugged her.

"What is all this?" When I hear my father's voice, I sob and run to him. He catches me in his big arms, and I finally see how much he's aged. His beard is salt and pepper now. I'm sure the hair on his head is the same, but it's covered with the cowboy hat that he puts on as soon as he starts his day. "There's my girl," he says softly, and I know that with them, nothing will be able to touch me. They will protect me until the end.

"Okay, enough of that," my mother says, and I look back at her, and she has her arm around Olivia, who wipes her own tears. "We need to get these two fed. The wind is going to take them away."

"God, she's been cooking for a week. You would think it's going to be your last meal," he whispers in my ear, and I laugh and use my sleeve to wipe my nose.

"I'll go set the table. You get the bags," my mother says to my father, who just nods, but I shake my head.

"No can do," Olivia says. "I got my bag." She goes to the car and opens the trunk.

"She is going to kill herself," my father says as we watch Olivia take out her massive luggage that took both me and her to lift. I try not to laugh at her when she drops it on her foot.

"Motherfucker!" she yells and then looks at my parents. "Sorry," she hisses out. I see her grab the handle, and she tries to roll it over the gravel, but it gets stuck on the rocks. All of a sudden, Casey storms past us and straight to Olivia.

My brother is all that and a bag of chips as the girls in town say. "Why haven't y'all helped the lady?" His Southern voice booms, making Olivia look up, and her mouth hangs open. My brother is six foot three, and he's six foot three of muscle. He's in his regular faded blue jeans, cowboy boots, and a white T-shirt. His skin is bronzed, and unlike my father, he doesn't wear his cowboy hat unless he has clients coming over to check out the horses. "I got it, sugar," he says, smiling at her, and I roll my eyes. His smile lights up his whole face, and it's gotten him out of enough trouble over the years that it's annoying to me.

Olivia just looks up and still says nothing. "Don't tell me the cat's got your tongue." He winks at her, and I have to save her.

"That's enough, Romeo," I say to him, and he looks over

his shoulder. "Don't waste all that charm on Olivia. She's immune to it."

He runs his hand through his hair, making his arm flex. "Is that so?"

"Um," Olivia says. "Um."

"Goodness gracious," my mother mumbles. "Casey, you get the bags upstairs." She looks at my father. "Let's get the food on the table."

"Mom," I say, and she holds up her hand.

"Don't even mom me. You are skin and bones."

I shake my head. "I'm not."

"Hush up," my mother says. She turns on her sneakers and walks up the two steps, letting the door slam behind her.

"Um, Kallie," Olivia says from beside me when Casey walks up the steps and my father holds the screen door open for him. "Is that your brother?"

"Yup," I say, nodding my head. "That would be Casey."

"Why have I never heard about him or seen pictures of him?" she asks, and I put my hand up to my head.

"There is a picture in my bedroom of me on gradation day with my family," I say, and she tilts her head.

"That man is not in that picture." She points at the door. "He's married, right? He has a herd of children." We walk slowly to the front door.

I throw my head back and laugh. "I don't even know what to say to that, but the answer is no. He is not one to be tied down."

"Good God," she says. The smell of my mother's cooking hits me right away, and my mouth waters.

I pull open the screen door, and my feet don't move from the spot. It's almost the same from when I left. All that's changed are the paint colors. But when I walk inside, the pictures lining the wall are all there. Pictures from our childhood to high school and then college. There are a couple from

Christmas, but I'm not in those, and my hand comes out on its own, and I trace the frame. "See, he's in this picture," Olivia says from beside me. "He's definitely not in the one in your room."

"He's just in the back, and you don't notice him." I laugh, shaking my head. Then I hear Casey walking upstairs and then jogging down the steps. "Definitely not," Olivia says from beside me.

"I set her up in my old room," he says and then looks at Olivia. "I can give you a tour later if you want."

"NO!" I shout out the same time Olivia says, "Sure."

"Goodness gracious," my mother says, coming out of the kitchen wiping her hands on the apron she is now wearing. "Why the yellin'?"

"Nothing, Ma," Casey says. He walks past us, and I look at Olivia who watches him like he's her last meal on earth.

"We have a pact," I say.

"What pact?" She looks over at me.

"We aren't allowed to date each other's brother. It's a universal thing really. Friends are not allowed to date the other's siblings."

"I don't have a brother," she informs me, "but if I did, and he looked like that, I would let you date him. I mean, date is a strong word since I gave up on dating, but I would let you find out if he wears boxers or briefs." She points at Casey.

"It's boxer briefs," I say. "There, now no need to find out."

"He could make me forget," she says, and I groan. "Fine, fine."

We walk into the kitchen area, and it's just like it's always been. All six burners on the range have a pot of them. The long wooden table in front of the big island also has food on it with a vase of fresh flowers in the middle. Something my father always does is bring her fresh flowers every single Friday. "It smells so good," I say to my mother, and she just smiles.

"Go wash up and then have a seat." She points at the bathroom, and Olivia and I both go wash our hands. When we come back, the table is set, and Casey and my father are bringing plates to the table.

"How many people are coming?" Olivia whispers, and I shrug.

"Everything is bigger in the South," I say, walking to the table.

"Heehaw to that," Casey says and then looks at Olivia. "Saved you a seat, darlin'."

"You." I point at Casey. "Stop that right now. We have a pact."

"It's null and void." He smirks. "Has been since you left."

"How many?" I ask him, thinking of how many of my friends he's hooked up with and broke their hearts.

"A gentleman never kisses and tells." He sits down, and I look around.

"I don't see any gentlemen here," I say, grabbing my own chair and sitting down. "You." I point at Olivia. "Come sit here next to me."

"Would you relax? I can handle myself." She pulls out the chair and sits down. "Oh my gosh, is that fried chicken?"

"Yup," I say when my mother puts down the plate of chicken. "That's chicken fried steak." I point at the plate next to the chicken. "That's shrimp and grits. And then collard greens, biscuits with gravy you can also put on the chicken fried steak, and cornbread."

"I'm going to be a million pounds when I leave here," Olivia says, looking at all the food. I'm about to grab a piece of chicken when a phone rings, and we both look at each other. The panic in her eyes is apparent, and she almost bolts from the table. Casey's eyes fly to hers and then mine as he pulls his phone out of his back pocket. He looks down and then looks at me.

"'Bout fucking time you took your head out of your ass," he says and looks at me and then my parents as he pushes away from the table. "I was calling to give you a heads-up." He walks out of the room.

"No one will touch you here," my father says softly, and Olivia grabs her napkin and dabs her eyes. I don't say anything when Casey comes back into the house, the door slamming behind him.

I watch him toss his phone on the counter. "Well, it's safe to say people know you're back."

Five

JACOB

"Is this going to be a problem?" Savannah asks, and I shake my head.

"Ethan, say bye to Mom," I tell my son who walks over to his mom and reaches up to give her a hug.

"Love you, kiddo," she says and then she looks at me. "Can you call me later?"

"Will do." I nod at her. Having Kallie back in town is fucking with me, and I saw her for point seven seconds. I feel shifted, and I hate it. I get Ethan in the truck and buckle him in. "Eat what your mom packed you." I point at the lunch bag that he put on the seat when he got in.

After closing the door, I try my hardest to slow my heart rate, but I know I have to call Casey. I get into the truck and drive over to the football field. I get Ethan out of his seat, then grab his equipment from the back. "You finish your food?" I ask, and he just nods. "Have a good game," I say and kiss his head.

I wait for him to get to his coach before I grab my phone out of my pocket and call Casey, who answers after three agonizing rings.

"'Bout fucking time you took your head out of your ass," he says.

"Kallie's back in town." I don't even bother acknowledging his previous statement. There are a lot of things I feel for the whole family, but I can only step in the ring with Casey.

"I was calling to give you a heads-up." I hear a chair scrape, and I wonder if he's at home with her.

"Cut the bullshit," I hiss. "The last thing you would ever do was help me."

"Wasn't me who had a kid with someone else, was it?" He always hits below the belt. "Either way, I just wanted you to know she's back."

"I saw that," I say, then my voice goes soft. "She saw me already. I was in front of the station with Ethan." I don't know why I say it, but I do. I say it because I know that if the roles were reversed and I saw her with a child she had with someone else, I would need to bury my sorrows in a bottle of whiskey. Fuck, just the thought of it makes me sick.

"Fuck," he hisses. "Needless to say, I think it's a good idea if you both avoid each other."

"Works for me," I say and disconnect the call. I walk over to the stands and take my usual spot. A couple of parents wave at me, and some of the dads walking by stop and shake my hand.

My foot moves up and down with nerves, and I force myself not to go back to the past. I force myself not to think about how the whole family kept her from me. I force myself not to go back down the black hole of what happened when she left.

"Hey." I spot Beau climbing the bleachers, and he sits next to me.

"Hey there, future mayor," I joke with him. He's dressed in slacks and a white button-down rolled up at the sleeves.

"Very funny," he says, shaking his head. "What's the scoop?"

"Kallie is back in town," I say, looking at the field and avoiding his stare. Out of everyone, he is the only one who saw how hard it was for me when Kallie left. The night of prom, we both sat in my barn and drank until we passed out. He didn't even question how I could do that to Kallie. He didn't ask me anything; he just drank with me. When I went to Kallie the next day and begged to see her, he had my back. When I sat in front of her house for three days straight watching for her, he was right next to me. He was also there the day I became a father. He has been a better brother to me than my actual brother.

"What do you mean when you say Kallie is back?" he mumbles and looks around to make sure he didn't say it too loud. The thing is, the gossip mill spreads faster than the speed of lightning in a small town.

"Pretty much exactly that. Kallie is back," I say.

"To stay?" He asks the question that has run through my mind over and over again. Not that I care because I couldn't care less. But I'm sure it's easier to hate her when she isn't in front of my face every single day.

"No fucking clue. Casey called me today, but I told him to fuck off." I swallow. "Then she stops in front of the station."

"Wow," he says, running his hands through his hair. "This is insane. Kallie."

"Yup." That's the last thing I say before Ethan jogs onto the field, and the football game starts. The whole time, my head is spinning.

"You need me to come over?" Beau asks when the game finishes, and he high-fives Ethan when he comes out with a popsicle.

"No," I say, "I'm putting him to bed, and then I'm crashing. I've been on duty for the past four days."

"Well," he says, stopping next to his brand-new BMW. "Let me know if you change your mind."

"Will do," I say, opening the truck door and buckling Ethan in. I make it home and get him in the shower when my phone rings again, and I see it's my mother.

"Please tell me it isn't true," my mother hisses as soon as I answer the phone. My mother has been a rock, my rock. She is the one who held my hand when I told my father that Savannah was pregnant. She never judged me or asked me how I could have done this to Kallie. She refused to let the town win when they basically shunned me for cheating on Kallie.

"Hey, Mom," I say, going to the fridge and grabbing a beer. I twist the cap off and take a long pull.

"I can't even believe she is showing her face after all this time." She slams something. "After everything that you've been through."

"Mom," I say, "it's fine."

"It's not fine. She broke your heart and didn't even give you a chance to explain."

"I mean, I did get another woman pregnant," I say. I hate having to defend Kallie; that stopped being my job when she stormed out of town without looking back.

"Well." My mother's voice goes soft. "You made one mistake. You had no choice but to be there for Savannah. She was having your child."

I take another pull, this time making my stomach burn.

"It's fine, Mom," I say. "It'll be fine."

"Yeah, it'll be fine when she leaves town again," she hisses. "I have to go. I'm in the middle of baking."

"Oh, fuck," I say. She always does this when she gets nervous or she is angry about something or she is heartbroken. When Kallie left town, she baked every day for a week. When her friendship with Charlotte, Kallie's mom, ended, she baked twice a day. When my father died, she baked three times a day. We had to buy her another freezer so she could fill it. "Mom, I swear it's going to be fine."

"I know," she says. "Bring Ethan over here tomorrow after school. He loves to bake with me."

"Will do, Mom," I say and disconnect. I get Ethan into bed and sit by his bed while he says his prayers, and then I read him a goodnight story. I know that it's going to end soon, so I'm taking full advantage of it.

I kiss his head and walk out of the room, closing the door a bit, and then walk through the quiet house. A house my parents bought for me as soon as the shock of me becoming a father set in. I, of course, refused, and they insisted even more. "It's for our grandson."

I make sure that the dim light over the stove is on and go into my room to my private shower. I hang my head and let the hot water cascade around me, my mind going back to the past.

I opened the front door, my heart crushed and my body in pain as I thought about the fact that what was supposed to be the best night of our lives was now the worst. My father was sitting on the couch with his arm around my mother as she cried into a tissue in her hand. She'd obviously already got the news. The phone started ringing again, and they both ignored it.

"You have to tell me it's a lie," my mother sobbed. "It can't be true."

My father's eyes never left mine, and it was like he knew the truth.

"It'll be fine." My father tried to soothe her. "It'll all be okay."

"I'm sorry." Those were the only words I could actually say.

A week later, my dad found me in the barn and grabbed a bottle of whiskey. He put one glass down and then another and then filled it. He looked at me, and I grabbed the glass and swallowed the amber liquid. It burned all the way down, but I only felt a sliver of pain. "That isn't your child." He wasn't asking me; he was telling me. "There is no way that is your child."

"How?" I asked him, but I wasn't surprised he knew the truth. It was why he was so good at his job. "You can't say anything."

"Not my story to tell," my father said, pouring another shot. "I just hope you know what you're doing."

"I know that I have to protect that child." I took another shot, hissing, "My child."

I turn off the water and shake my head. These flashbacks are not going to change or help anything.

I slip on my boxers and the pants that I wear when Ethan is here. He walked in one morning and my cock was at full salute, and we had to have an in-depth conversation about how it gets so big and what to do with it.

I'm just slipping into bed when I hear a soft knock on the door, and I stand here, not sure if it's in my head or not. But then I hear it again, and my heart starts to beat faster. It starts to beat frantically when I walk closer and closer. I open the door, and my heart drops or maybe it crushes. I don't know why I expected it to be Kallie. I don't know why I even care.

"Sorry for coming over without calling first," Savannah says, walking into my house, and I close the door behind her. "I just ..." She takes a deep breath and walks into the living room. I look at her, and see she's wearing her blue jeans and a tight top. Don't get me wrong, she's beautiful, but I can't look past everything we've been through. We even had a talk when she gave birth about moving in together and trying to be a family, but I just couldn't take that step. "This is crazy."

"I'm sorry. I'm past the point of tired," I say. "What are you talking about?"

"I'm talking about the fact that Kallie just showed up in town." She speaks quietly so as not to wake Ethan up. "I'm talking about the fact that the last time you saw her was prom."

"I know exactly when the last time I saw her, Savannah. I was there," I remind her.

"You promised me," she says, and I hold up my hand.

"I have never once told anyone your secret. Not to my parents, not to my brother, not even to Beau, so don't even start."

She wipes away a tear. "I'm sorry. Talk in the town has already started. The bar was full tonight. On a Wednesday," she says. When she gave birth, she bought the town bar and vamped it up. I never asked her how she got the money or what she had to do for it. I don't want to know. All I need to know is that she is the best mother there is, and Ethan thrives with both of his parents.

"Give it a couple of days," I say. "Something else will happen, and then it'll be old news."

"It's taken seven years for people to be nice to me." She sits down on the couch. "Seven years for me to finally walk into the grocery store without being pointed at as the 'harlot' who stole you away from the town's princess."

"The only thing that matters is that the town loves Ethan," I remind her. "How they feel about me or you is not an issue."

She puts her head back. "Yeah, I know. I just wanted to make sure we were on the same page," she says, getting up. "I'll get out of your hair."

She walks to me. "He has a spelling test tomorrow. Just go over the words in the car."

"Will do," I say, and she leans up to kiss my cheek.

"Thank you," she says and walks out of the house. I walk

out the door and watch her drive away. Stopping in the middle of my porch, I sit down and look at the sky.

"What the hell are you doing back in town, Kallie?" I ask the universe, and I expect to get an answer, but instead, all I hear is the silence. It's always the silence that greets me.

Six

KALLIE

I toss and turn in bed even though I'm exhausted and fell asleep five minutes after getting out of my shower. I wake suddenly and just lie here, my heartbeat going through the motions, just as it has been for the past eight years.

My room has stayed the same since I left, the only things gone are the pictures I had of me and Jacob all over my room. I don't even think about all the times he climbed into my bed after my parents were asleep and just held me. Memories that I locked away and somehow forgot now come crashing back, making it hard for me to breathe. I get up, sitting at the end of the bed, trying to collect my breaths. In through the nose, out through the mouth. I get up and go to my luggage that sits open on the floor, looking like it just exploded everywhere. I refuse to wear any of the clothes I left here. I left them here for a reason, so there is no way I'm going to put them on now. In fact, I'm packing them up tomorrow and taking them to the church so they can give them away.

I pull on my yoga pants and put on a sweater. Sliding open my door, I slowly wait for the creak that used to come when it opened halfway. This time, it doesn't make any noise as I slip out of my room and go down the stairs. The light in the kitchen is on like always, and a plate of muffins sits on the island right next to the vase of flowers. I walk over to the door and grab my running shoes. After I put them on, I slip out of the door and walk to the barn. I stop and listen for it, waiting to hear a car horn honk or backfire or a siren blaring somewhere, but instead, it's nothing but crickets. The light from the stars leads me to the barn, and I slide the big metal door open, just like I used to do all those years ago when I couldn't sleep.

The lights are on dim in each of the stalls as I walk down the concrete path in the middle of the barn. I hear the horses in their stalls as I make my way over to the one I know is mine. Lady Princess is written on the outside of the stall. She comes over to the opening, her brown coat still as bright as when I got her ten years ago. My sweet sixteen present from my father.

"Hey, girl," I say, holding my hand out to her so she can smell me. She knocks my hand with her nose. "Sorry I left you," I say, rubbing down her muzzle. "I heard you were pissed."

"She was." When I hear that from behind me, I yelp, scaring her and a couple of the other horses.

"Jesus H," I say. Looking behind me, I find Casey standing there in just jeans with a rifle in his hand. "Casey, what in the fuck?" I shriek.

"You almost got yourself shot," he says. "What in the fuck are you doing out here at one in the morning?"

"How in the hell did you know I was here?" I ask, still trying to get my heart to calm down.

"You triggered the alarm," he says, pointing at the door. "I have it set up in my house. It tells me everything."

"Well, would you look at that." I smile at him. "Can you help me saddle her?" I ask. "And can you please put that gun away?"

He puts the gun down and walks over to the far end of the barn, returning with my saddle. "When I found out you were coming home, I had her cleaned up and shined," he says. Opening the stall door, he holds up his hand, calling Lady. She slowly comes out and waits for him to put the saddle on her. He ties it tight around her belly and then steps back. "You need help mounting her?" His voice comes out smooth, and I cringe.

"One, I can't even with that sentence," I say, pushing him aside, "and two, I don't need you to help me do anything but open the garage door."

"Want company?" he asks me when I walk over to Lady and pet the side of her neck. I shake my head. "Okay. Well, leave the saddle on her, and I'll take care of it when I come in," he says, grabbing the shotgun and then walking out.

"You could put on boots and get a gun, but you couldn't put on a shirt?" I ask, and he shrugs.

"I was hoping it was Olivia," he says, and I groan. "Be safe." He opens the barn door, and I put one foot in the stirrup and swing my leg over to sit on her. She backs up a couple of steps and then slowly she walks forward. "Be careful. She gets pissy when you try to guide her too much, and last time, she tried to buck Mom off."

"She's good," I say, holding the reins in both of my hands. "It's like riding a bike." Using my foot, I make her start to trot. "That's a good girl."

She takes me down the path we always used to go, down the path where I spent more and more time with her as I got older, knowing I was going to leave her eventually. What I wasn't intending was to go away for so long. My head is not even paying attention to where she is going until I hear the creek. She walks alongside the creek where I used to meet Jacob. I make Lady stop at the tree and get off, then lead her over to the creek so she can drink for a bit. I walk to the tree where he carved our names into the trunk. I expect to see our names still there except they're not there. There is nothing. It's like someone cut it out of the tree. My hand comes up and traces the smooth wood. I look at the tree next to it, thinking I might have gotten the wrong tree, but it's not there either. I look around in the darkness, thinking I came to the wrong spot, but then I spot the rock he made Beau carry up here. The big boulder where we would sit while we spoke about the future. I walk over to it, and the memory of us sitting on that rock comes rushing forward. He'd sit behind me, and I'd press my head back on his shoulder, looking up at him. My hand on his cheek, my heart so full.

"Do you love me?" I used to ask him every single time.

"My heart doesn't beat without you." He used to say each time.

It knocks me to my knees, and my wails and sobs echo in the quiet night. My hand goes to my chest, the pain as intense as if it was yesterday. I sit with my back to the stone, trying to make sense of everything. When did it go wrong? How did it go wrong? How did I not see it? How did I not feel it? How? *How?*

Lady grazes near me, and when the sun starts to come up, I finally get up and walk over to her. My body feels beaten, but I get on Lady and we make our way back home. This time, I go as slow or as fast as she wants. When I approach the barn, the door opens, and I see Casey coming out with a cup of coffee in his hand. He's already dressed in jeans, his boots, and this time, a shirt. "I was about to send out a search party," he says, and his eyes meet mine.

"Just going down memory lane," I say, getting off Lady and handing him the reins. "There is a rock I want moved."

"Is it by the tree that Jacob tried to cut down?" he asks, and my head snaps back.

"Mom is up and found your friend Olivia asleep outside on the porch swing," Casey tells me, and my eyes open.

"She doesn't sleep ever since ..." I don't tell him the rest because it's not my story to tell, and if she wants to tell him, then that's on her.

"What is it with you city folks and sleeping in beds?" he asks, and I just shrug. "Tell Mom I'll be in for breakfast in twenty."

"You are thirty, and your mother still cooks you breakfast?" I shake my head.

"One thing at a time." He laughs. "It took me two years to actually move out to my own house."

"I can't wait to see it," I say.

"Tonight after dinner, I'll give you and Olivia the tour." He winks at me, and I turn to walk back to the house. My sneakers are filled with dust now. I open the porch door and quietly enter the house.

The smell of bacon and coffee hits me right away. "Morning," I say. Yawning, I walk over to the coffeepot and grab a white mug. I fill it to the brim and then take a sip. "So good."

"Since when do you drink your coffee black?" my mother asks as she mixes eggs in a big bowl.

"Since I saw how much fat is in half and half," I say, and she just shakes her head. "Where's Olivia?"

"Well, she got up at around three this morning, and then I heard her go outside. When I woke up at five, she was sleeping outside on the porch swing. Then she got up and did some Namaste things on the lawn."

"Yoga." I try not to laugh at my mother. "I want to swing by the church if we can today." Her eyes fly up at me.

"Of course." She tries to hide her surprise that I want to leave the house.

"Good," I say. Walking upstairs with my coffee, I go take another shower. When I get out, I slip on a white tank top and fumble around for a pair of jeans but none of them are what I'm looking for. I open my drawer where I used to keep my jeans and grab my overalls. I smile when I think about how crazy it is that this is now the style again. I slip into them, and I roll up the bottoms and then slip on my white Converse shoes. I grab the cup of coffee and head downstairs, hearing voices.

"You can't go out wearing that." I hear Casey, and I roll my eyes.

"Why not?" Olivia asks, and I walk in and see what she is wearing. She has her tight white jeans that mold her and make her ass look amazing with a white tank top cut low in the front, showing her cleavage.

"You'll stick out like a sore thumb," he says, and she laughs.

"I have a jacket," she says, walking to the chair and putting on her beige jacket with big gold buttons.

"Yeah, that's much better," he says, hiding his smile. "I'm sure Kallie has some shoes for you to borrow."

"Oh, no," Olivia says, going to the front door and grabbing her high heel sandals. Putting them on just makes her whole outfit sexy.

"No fucking way," Casey says, and my mother laughs.

"Watch your language, young man." She points at my brother. "Honey." She turns to Olivia. "You might be a bit overdressed. But if you want to wear that …"

"I think it's too much," I say, and she looks at me. "Definitely leave the jacket off." I try to roll my lips when I hear Casey groan and bang his head on the table.

"I'm going to have to sleep in my truck tonight," he says, pushing off the table and carrying his plate to the sink. "Thanks, Ma," he says, kissing her cheek. Then he comes over to me. "Try not to get the gossip going, would ya?" he says and then walks over to Olivia. My mother and I both watch him. "Have a good day, sugar." He leans in and kisses her on the mouth, stunning her and us. "See you later," he says and walks out the door.

"What in the heavens?" my mother says, and I look at Olivia, who just puts her hand to her lips.

"Does everyone in the country just kiss you?" she asks, and I shake my head.

"Not unless they want to get shot," I say, and my mother laughs. I eat a bit of breakfast and help my mother clean up. When we're finished, I grab a couple of bags and head upstairs while Olivia opens her computer and starts answering emails.

"I'm ready," I say when I walk down the stairs with four bags stuffed with clothes.

"I just finished making lunch," my mother says, wiping her hands. "Why don't we go? I have to get a couple of things at the butcher."

We get into my mother's truck, and I fasten my seat belt and look back at Olivia in the back, putting on her designer sunglasses out of her Yves Saint Laurent purse.

"Here goes nothing," I say under my breath when my mother pulls out of the driveway.

Seven

JACOB

"Let's go, kiddo!" I yell down the hall while I pour another cup of coffee, this time in a to-go cup. I thought I would sleep like the dead, but instead, all I did was sit outside looking at the sky. I have no idea if I was looking for a sign or what, but tossing and turning in bed got old, so I went outside and spent the night lying on my porch couch just listening to the silence and looking at the blinking stars. When the sky started to get pink, I got up and ran on the treadmill that I have set up at home.

"Dad!" I hear Ethan yell. "I can't find my bag." I shake my head. My son would lose his head if it wasn't attached to his body. I walk to one of the chairs at the kitchen table and see it there.

"It's in the kitchen," I say, and then he comes running into the kitchen wearing shorts and a T-shirt. I look down at myself and see we are almost dressed the same; the only difference is I have a baseball hat on. "You ready?" I ask. He grabs the toast I put on a plate on the table, then nods.

He picks up his sweater and backpack and forgets to grab his lunch box. I grab it from the counter with my keys and walk out with him, slamming the door behind me as I watch Ethan get into the truck and buckle himself in. I open his door, and he looks at me with a what now look. I hold up his lunch box in my hand, and he smiles. "Oh, I forgot that," he says, smirking and holding out his hand for it.

"Yeah, you forgot that," I say and close the door, getting into the front seat. The drive to school is max ten minutes. I pull up in the drop-off lane, and I'm greeted by one of Ethan's teachers, Jana, wearing the drop-off vest. She opens the back door to get Ethan out.

"Good morning, Ethan," she says softly and smiles at him. Her eyes meet mine, and she smiles bigger. "Morning, Jacob." I nod at her. It's no secret that I'm the town's single dad. It's also no secret that I haven't dated anyone really in the past eight years. It's also no secret that every single woman in the town is waiting for me to take the leap, especially Jana.

"Morning, Jana." I smile at her and then wonder maybe if I should ask her out.

"Bye, Dad," Ethan says. He gets out of the truck, and Jana closes the door as soon as he's out. Pulling off, I call Beau, who answers right away and sounds like he's panting. "What are you doing?"

"Running," he says, and I shake my head.

"How can you answer when you're running?" I ask, heading back home.

"It's called AirPods, old man." He laughs. "What can I do for you?" Through it all, Beau has been my best friend. He really stood by my side when Kallie left, but more importantly, he was there when my father died. More than my brother, who only came into town for two days and then ran away before the sun set after burying him.

"Do you think I should ask Jana out?" I ask, and he laughs.

"Jana," he repeats the name, "the teacher who teaches

45

your son?" I roll my eyes. "'Cause that sounds like a great idea. How do you think the next parent-teacher conference will go after you dump her two dates in?"

"What if I don't dump her?' I ask. "I mean, she's cute."

"Yeah, that's always something that you want to hear from a date. You're cute."

"What am I supposed to say?" I ask. "And first of all, who are you to talk? When was the last time you went on a date?"

"Two weeks ago," he says without skipping a beat. "I had a date for a charity event."

I groan. "That's not a date." Shaking my head, I say, "That's your mother playing matchmaker."

"Same thing," he tells me. "I don't want to date. I have to focus on the mayor's office, and dating isn't up there on my list of shit to do."

I pull up to my house, and I spot Casey there, leaning against his truck as he waits for me. "What the fuck?"

"What happened?" he asks.

"Casey is here," I say, stopping my truck and turning it off. "I'll call you back."

"Don't get yourself arrested, Jacob. I am not in office yet, so the only thing I can do is bail you out," he says, and I disconnect the call, getting out of the truck.

"What are you doing here?" I ask, cutting through the bullshit, and he looks at me.

"It seems there is something on my property that needs to be moved," he says, and I look at him with a confused look on my face no doubt. Why would I give a shit what is on his property, and why would I need to know? "There is a rock that seems to be in the wrong place, and I'm just letting you know that I'm having it moved." I don't know why it feels like he just kicked me in the stomach, but it does. "I'm guessing by the look on your face that you know what rock I'm talking about."

I put my game face on. "Fuck if I care what you do with that rock. Toss it in the creek. Blow it up for all I care."

"Perfect. I just assumed since you tried to cut down the tree right next to it, you might want to know." He looks at me, putting his hands in his back pockets. We've never actually been friends since he was the same age as my brother, but we always got along. Well, we did until he hid Kallie from me and then refused to tell me where she was.

I shake my head. "Don't care."

"Sure," he says, turning and getting into his truck. "You keep telling yourself that, and maybe one day, you'll actually believe yourself."

"What does that mean?" I say, and it's his turn now to shake his head.

"I'm not spelling shit out for you," he says, starting the truck. "The only thing I know is my sister is finally back at home, and I'm going to do what I need to do to make sure she comes back often."

"Again," I say, "don't care."

"Again," he mimics me, "you keep telling yourself that."

"I wasn't the one who left without looking back!" I shout.

"Wasn't her who got knocked up by another guy!" He throws it in my face, and I just shake my head. "Take care, Jacob." He pulls out of my driveway, and I want to shout and tell him to fuck off. I want to shout and tell him that he knows fucking nothing, but I do what I've been doing for the past eight years. I keep the secret to myself, burying it deep. I walk into my house and close the door. Tossing my phone on the counter, I walk straight to my bedroom.

I collapse on the bed and turn to look out the window at the trees in the distance. My thoughts go back to the last time I went to the rock.

"What exactly did you want me to come for?" Beau asked as we walked through the woods toward Kallie's property. I

47

parked as close as I could, then got out and grabbed the chainsaw.

"I need to do something and figured that you had nothing else to do." I laughed and walked along the creek. Water slowly worked itself downstream. The sound of birds chirping mixed with the sounds of water trickling.

"I don't think anything that you have to do with a chainsaw is a good idea," he said as he continued walking. Finally, I walked over the hill and saw the lone rock right next to five elm trees. The sun made its way through the leaves, shining on the rock like a spotlight.

Even though I wanted to go sit on the rock and see if I could still feel her all around me, I ignored it. Instead, I walked straight to the tree where I had carved our names into one day. We were lying with her head on my chest and my arms around her. My hand came out, and I traced the letters with my finger, lost in the thought of her again, but I was done. It was enough or at least that was what I thought. I pulled the string and the chainsaw roared to life. I was about to cut the fucking tree down when Beau shouted.

"Are you out of your mind?" he said once I shut off the chainsaw. "You can't cut down this tree."

I looked around. "Why not?"

"Well, for one, I think it's against the law since it's, you know ..." He looked around now. "Not your property, and two, because it's not a good fucking idea."

"My name is on it"—I pointed at him, and he rolled his eyes—"so I think that makes it mine." I knew I sounded stupid, and I knew that it was not my best idea, but I just wanted to bury another piece of us.

"Well, I think that Casey would not agree with you," he said, and then I looked down and thought about it. I knew he was right, so instead of cutting down the tree, I cut my name off *it. I expected to be gone before anyone saw us, but then I heard a galloping horse approaching. I saw him through the trees as he guided his horse toward us.*

"What in the ever-loving fuck are you doing?" he said as soon as he got the horse to stop beside me.

"Nothing." Beau tried to calm the situation.

"I want my name off your tree." I pointed at the tree.

"Did you think you would be able to cut down a fucking tree and me not notice?" he asked, shaking his head, then he looked at Beau. "Make sure he doesn't cut more than he needs to." He kicked his horse and took off.

"I'm right here," I yelled at his retreating back, "son of a bitch." I started the chainsaw, and in five minutes, our names were in little pieces on the grass. All that was there now was the light brown bark. My hands came out, and I traced it with my finger. Blank, fresh, new.

"Knock, knock, knock." I hear the front door open, and I sit up, my mind coming back to the present. "Hello?" I hear my mother's voice, and then she finally finds me. "There you are. Why are you in bed?"

"I was just lying down. I didn't really sleep last night," I say and avoid the sadness in her eyes. "What's up?"

"I have a couple of errands to run, and I was hoping that you would come with me. Maybe we can have lunch." She smiles, and I look at her.

"I was hoping to just relax," I say, and she frowns at me. "But yeah, let's go shopping. I need to get some things at the grocery store anyway."

She claps her hands together. "Oh, goody."

I get up and follow her out of the house, getting into my truck. "Where do you want to go first?"

"How about we go get something to eat, and then we can tackle the errands? I need to go to a couple of places."

I smile at her and make my way to the town diner. The whole time, I try to forget about the memories that are suddenly crashing in on me.

Eight

KALLIE

I knew coming home would be hard, and I have to admit I thought it was going to be bad. I wasn't expecting to miss everything so much once I finally saw it again.

Just the smell of going into the church brought me back to my best memories of growing up. All those memories included Jacob, but it also included my memories. "How have I been gone for eight years, yet the town looks like it did when I left?"

"Things change," my mother says, pulling into the parking lot. "It's just not an apparent change." I get out of the truck and wait for Olivia to get out of the truck and look around.

"I don't think I've seen so much green in my whole life." She smiles at me. "And not once did I hear a siren." She puts her head back and smells the air. "And what is that fresh smell?"

"I can tell you it isn't pollution," I joke with her, and the three of us walk from the parking lot into the grocery store. My mother was right. Things change; they just aren't apparent. The inside of the grocery store looks the same, but it's not. They have a little section when you come in that has all the natural items.

"Oh, there is my section," Olivia says, walking toward the one shelf.

I walk to my left to grab a cart, and I'm surprised that the metal carts have now been replaced with the red plastic ones. We go through the fruits and vegetables first. My mother picks up some apples, and then I grab a couple of things, putting them in the basket. We stop at the butcher counter, and the man shrieks when he sees me. "Well, I'll be." He smiles at me, walking over, and I recognize him except his hair is whiter now on the side, and the hair on top of his head is gone. "Ain't you a sight for sore eyes?" he says, and I look at him. His white jacket is just like he always wears with a big white apron on in front of him with blood stains.

"Mr. Johnson." I smile back at him. "It's so great to see you."

He nods. "You were very missed," he says, looking over at my mother who stands there beaming with pride. She puts her hands around my shoulder. "Especially by that lady."

"I know." I look down at the brown floor. "But I'm back."

"That's good to hear," he says, and then he looks at my mother, who places her order with him. "Why don't you guys go do your shopping, and I'll bring this to you when I'm done?"

We go through the aisles, stopping every second step as someone I know welcomes me home. I get so many hugs it feels like I've been gone forever. "How does it feel?" Mrs. Henderson asks, and I look at her. "To be back home. Especially after everything—"

I don't make her finish. "It's great to be back." I cut her off because I don't want to feed into the gossip mill.

"I'm sure it is, dear," she says, patting my hand on the cart. "You just need to gain a few, and you'll be good to go."

"It was so nice seeing you," my mother says with a tight smile. "See you Sunday at church."

"See you then," she says, pushing her cart and walking away.

"Well, that wasn't bad." I laugh to my mother and start to walk forward when I stop in my tracks, and I want to crawl into a hole. My mother stops next to me, not sure, and then she looks up and sees Cristine, Jacob's mother, walking down the aisle looking around. When she finally spots us, her smile drops from her face, and in its place is a stare of death.

"You have got to be fucking kidding me," she says loudly, and I look around now, wondering just how big this show-down is going to be. I see that it's just the three of us, and I have to wonder if it's because people know and are avoiding this aisle.

"Crissy, don't you dare," my mother says, stepping in front of me to shield me.

"Don't I dare?" She pushes her cart closer to us, then she walks around and comes face-to-face with us. I hold my mother's hand and stand beside her.

"Don't I dare?" I say now. "Don't *I* dare?" I point at myself.

"You," she hisses and points at me. "You left without so much as a second thought. Do you know how broken you left him?" She says the last words, and I feel as if she slapped me in the face. I flinch back.

"He wasn't the only one who was left broken!" my mother shouts, and people around us now look at us. "You have no idea what she went through."

"How would we know? She never told anyone," Cristine says.

"Tell you?" I say softly, putting my arms around my mother. "I needed to tell you how your son destroyed me." I blink away the tears that are threatening to come no matter how much I fight them.

"She wasn't the one who changed anything, Crissy," my mother says, and she doesn't hide the tears. "I lost my daughter that day. You still have your son. Your son who is always around. You have your son and your grandson." I pull her closer to me, ignoring the pain when she says grandson. "So don't even think you got the short end of the stick."

"What the hell?" When I hear his voice, my eyes look up, and I'm stuck in place. My chest aches, my stomach falls, and my knees tremble. It's everything bombarding me at the same time—hatred, sadness, anger, and then love. The fucking love that I've felt for him for my whole life.

The tears that I fought so hard to hold back deceive me. One falls out, and I brush it away, hoping no one says anything. I look away from him, away from the way he looks at me.

"We were just leaving," I say and look at my mother. "Let's go." I'm about to turn around when I see Olivia looking around frantically and then calling my name.

"Kallie," she says, her chest rising and falling, and I notice her hands are shaking. "Our place was ransacked."

"What?" I ask and grab her hand.

"That was a detective. He called to let us know that someone had broken into our place and trashed it."

"Oh my God." I look at my mother. "We have to go." I look back at Olivia, who looks around her to make sure no one is pointing a camera at us.

"Let's go," my mother says. I turn to walk away, and then I feel his hand on my arm. I know it's his hand because I would know his touch in the dark. Glancing down at his fingers, I stand here for longer than I care to until his hand drops, and my mother looks back at him.

"What detective?" he asks. I take a deep breath and turn.

No matter how many times I thought about this moment, no matter how many times I role-played when I was drunk, nothing could have prepared me for being so close to him.

"This doesn't concern you," I say. "Nothing about me or my life concerns you." It's his turn now to take a step back, and I turn and walk out of the shop with Olivia by my side.

"Holy shit," Olivia says from beside me. "Holy shit, did you just tell him to fuck off but in a nice Southern way?"

"I have no idea what I said. The only thing I was trying to do was block his smell."

I pull open the truck door while my mother jumps into the front and makes sure we are all in before she pulls out of the grocery store parking lot. "We need to call your father," my mother says as she speeds through town, and all I can do is close my eyes. Close my eyes and hope to God that it's over, and I can leave here. That I never have to be that close to him again.

When we pull up to the house, my father and brother are walking around the house. They both look as if they are going to war with shotguns by their side.

"Oh my God," Olivia says from the back, "is that a shotgun?"

"No," I say, looking at her, "that's two shotguns."

I get out of the truck and wait for Olivia, who is still shaking. Trying to walk on the gravel in her heels, she almost trips, but surprise, Casey is there to catch her. "Careful, darlin'."

"Oh, would you please put that shit away?" I look at him. "You can't flirt with her. She's not in her right mind." I walk to the house, opening the door, and go straight to the cabinet in the living room where I know my father keeps his whiskey. "I need a drink."

My mother, Olivia, Casey, and my father watch me unscrew the bottle and take a pull from it. The amber liquid hits my tongue and then burns all the way down. I cough after the second gulp, and I think I might actually get sick.

"Okay, if you gals don't tell me what is going on, I don't know if I can calm this one down." My father uses his thumbs to motion to Casey, who stands there with his hands in his back pockets.

I hold out the bottle for Olivia, who walks over and takes it from me, spitting it out after a sip. "That's not whiskey." She's coughing and trying to catch her breath.

"It's like whiskey," I say, looking at the bottle. "It's just homemade."

"I can't breathe," she says through her coughing. "It burns so bad."

"Enough!" Casey shouts, and my mother sits on the couch and puts her hands in her lap as if she's going to be watching a movie. Olivia looks at me almost like she doesn't know what to say, and I just shrug.

"I think you just do it like a Band-Aid," I say. "Just come out with it."

"So I was in the gluten-free section at the grocery story, and my phone rings," she says. I look at Casey, and I almost laugh at the way he is bouncing on his heels. "It was from an unknown number, and I didn't answer the first time or the second, but then I got pissed."

"Darlin'," Casey says between clenched teeth, "can we go just a touch faster?"

"I'm trying, Casey," she says, and he just nods at her. If it was anyone else, I think he would have swore, which makes this even more interesting. "So, I pick up the phone with an angry tone." She motions with her phone to her ear. "And right when I'm about to tell the person I have no comment, he tells me his name is Detective Gonzalez with the LAPD."

"Oh my God," my father says.

"Well, it seems that our apartment was broken into,"

Olivia says, and her hands start to shake. "According to the detective, walls were damaged. Every single drawer was thrown on the floor. It was a mess. Every single thing we had there was broken or vandalized."

"Holy shit," I say, sitting up. "What do you mean everything?"

"Well, he sent me an email with pictures, and it's horrible," she says, handing me the phone so I can see the pictures. Our couches are shredded like people thought we were hiding something in it. The television is shattered. The kitchen cabinets are empty with all the plates on the floor in little pieces. The fridge was tipped over, my bedroom destroyed. They slashed my bed with the same knife as the couch. My drawers are thrown everywhere, and then I swipe to Olivia's, and I gasp. "It's everything I have ever had."

"It's in shreds," I say, but then I see the writing on the wall.

You'll get what's owed to you.

"What does that mean?" I ask Olivia, who now has tears streaming down her face. That's the straw that broke Casey's back because he storms over and grabs the phone from my hands to look at the pictures.

"Oh, fuck no," he says and then looks at my father. "We need to lock it down." My father just nods at him, and I'm about to ask him what he's talking about when there's a knock on the door.

My father looks at Casey, who grabs his shotgun and walks to the front door. He glances at my father, who is standing with his own gun in his hand, before he looks out the peephole. "Jesus fuck, what is with this day?" he says and opens the door, and for the second time today, I come face-to-face with the man I ran away from eight years ago.

Nine

JACOB

I don't know why I get tense when we walk into the grocery store. I don't even know why I do a sweep of the room, spotting a new blonde standing by the organic section. Right away, you know she's not from here.

"I have a couple of things to get, so I'll come find you when I'm done." my mother says, and she takes off. I try not to eye the blonde and think to myself maybe I can date her. She looks like she's new here, and she has no idea about my history in this town. No idea about the cloud that follows me. It's better now, but in the beginning, they would shake their heads when I would walk down the street. It got better when Ethan was born, and then when I took over as sheriff, it was all back to normal. Now, don't get me wrong. Some of the old timers still leer at me.

I push the cart down the aisles and avoid eye contact because each time I do look up, I have to have a ten-minute conversation with someone. And now that Kallie is back, I'm sure all the talk is going to be asking about what I am going to do. And then they will give me sad smiles and say, "That's okay, dear." I can't take it, and when I turn the corner, I spot the scene right away. Turning around, I see that everyone has stopped, and now I see why.

The showdown that everyone was probably waiting for. The showdown that will be spread all around town by the time dinner is served.

Kallie doesn't see me as I approach, and it gives me a couple of minutes to take her in. I want to say she looks the same, but she doesn't. I want to say her beauty doesn't blow me away, but I would be lying. I want to say my heart doesn't speed up just looking at her, but you can't mistake the galloping in my chest.

"How would we? She never thought to tell anyone," my mother hisses, and I look at Charlotte who has tears.

"Tell you?" Kallie says, her words coming out in almost a whisper. "I needed to tell you how your son destroyed me?" The words cut me off at the knees.

"She wasn't the one who changed anything, Crissy," Charlotte says to her, using my mother's nickname. The two of them were the best of friends, and then the rift started. "I lost my daughter that day. You still have your son. Your son who is always around. You have your son and your grandson." I see Kallie close her eyes when her mother says grandson. "So don't even think you got the short end of the stick."

"What the hell?" I say, cutting this off before it gets even uglier. Kallie's eyes come to mine, and I get lost in them just like I did every single time. I watch her movement as she turns to her mother, I watch her hands that I used to hold and kiss. When she slumps her shoulders, I want to grab her and put her over my shoulder and tell her everything. I want to tell her everything, and then suddenly, the anger from her leaving me comes in. The blonde from before comes down the aisle, and she is frantic and shaking. I look around, and I hear the two words that breaks me out of my trance. "The detective."

"Let's go," her mother says, and my hand shoots out

even before I can stop myself. I grab her arm, and the whole store sounds like it gasps in shock. Kallie doesn't turn around; the only thing she does is move her head down, looking at my hand on her arm. Her arm that feels different, smaller, frail.

"What detective?" I finally ask, looking around to see if I see anything out of place. It happens in slow motion, or at least it feels like that. She turns around, and now that she is so close, I can smell her again. I can see the little freckles on her nose.

"This doesn't concern you," she says. "Nothing about me or my life concerns you." I swear it's like she slaps me in the face, and I take a step back and watch her walk out of the store.

"I can't believe she is back to bring all this havoc to everyone," my mother says, but I look down at my hand that touched her, ignoring the tingling I feel. "Eight years and she just waltzes back into town."

"Mom." I say her name, and she looks at me. "That's enough." I look around, and everyone looks away, pretending that they just didn't watch the shitshow that went downhill. "Let's go, Mom."

She just nods, and we leave the basket in the middle of the store and walk out to my truck. My head is spinning. Why is a detective calling her? Why was the blonde shaking like a leaf? Why the fuck did Kallie really come home? I get in the truck and make my way back to my mother's house, neither of us saying anything. Pulling into her driveway, I turn off the truck. She reaches to the handle of the truck, and I finally say something. "What were you thinking?"

"I was thinking that life was finally good," she tells me. "People were finally forgetting about what happened."

"You think what you did in there helped anything at all?" I ask, and she looks down. "She was your best friend."

"And now she isn't." She wipes away a tear. "I have you, and I have my grandson."

"Mom." She looks up at me. "Don't do that again."

"Jacob, you can't be serious." She shakes her head. "You still love her."

"As much as I hate her," I say, looking out my window at the house I grew up in, "a piece of me will always love her." I swallow down the lump in my throat. "Can you get Ethan for me?"

"Of course," she says. "Why don't you do what you need to do and then come have dinner here?"

I nod, and she gets out of the truck. I pull out, and my car makes its way to Kallie's house. *I'm just doing my job*, I tell myself. *I'm just keeping my town safe.* My stomach is in my throat the whole time I'm on my way there.

Pulling into the driveway, I ignore all the memories that come crashing back. I block them out just as fast as they came in, and when I get out of the truck, the crunch of the rocks under my feet alerts them I'm here. I ring the bell and brace myself for what is to come.

When I hear the locks turn, I wait for it, and I'm not surprised when I see Casey with his shotgun in his hand. I know he'd love nothing more than to shoot me in the ass, but he wouldn't answer the door with it in his hand. Something is definitely going on.

"Not today," he says, and he tries to shut the door, but my hand comes out, and I block it from slamming.

He shakes his head and turns around, letting me walk into the house. His father stands there, leering at me with his own shotgun, and I have to think maybe coming into the enemy playpen was not the smartest idea I've ever had. "What the hell is going on?" I say, looking from Casey to Billy, and then I make the mistake of looking on the couch and seeing the blonde with tears running down her face. Kallie sits next to the blonde with her own tears in her eyes, and she looks away, wiping a tear away.

"It's not your concern," Casey says, and I shake my head. "Nothing that happens in this family is your concern."

"Casey," Billy says softly.

"You might not like me," I say, "but I don't like you either, so the feeling is mutual."

"Well, at least we agree on something," Casey says, smirking.

"What concerns me is what happens in my town," I say. "So if this"—I motion with my finger to the girls on the couch —"is bringing shit into my town, I need to know about it."

"We have it covered," Casey is fast to say, and then I look at Billy.

"He does have a point," Billy says, and now Kallie shoots off the couch.

"NO!" she shouts. She looks at me, and her tears are gone, and anger is there with something else. "I'm not having him do anything for me. We are going to leave." She looks at Olivia who looks at her and then at Casey.

"You can't leave," Charlotte says, dabbing her eyes. "You just got here, and we can keep you safe."

"You aren't going anywhere," Casey says, then looks at me.

Kallie walks to me, and I'm holding my breath. "This changes nothing," she spews at me. "The less I have to see you—"

I cut her off. "Trust me." I step toward her, and she doesn't move. "We can agree on that and one other thing. The faster this is done, the faster you can hightail it out of town." I look down, then up again, and I hope my look is that of hatred so she doesn't see how much I still hurt. "You're good at that." I stare into her eyes and try not to get lost in them.

"This isn't helping anyone," Billy says, and Kallie turns

away and walks to the bottle of whiskey on the table, taking a gulp. "You"—Billy points at her—"stop that."

"If I have to do this," Kallie says, using her fingers, "then I'm doing it drinking."

"I want a shot," the blonde says, and Casey speaks now.

"Darlin'." She looks up at him, and I wonder what the fuck is going on.

"You aren't the boss of the bottle," she tells him and reaches for it. Kallie just takes another gulp, and I want to tell her that it's enough.

"Oh, for the love of everything," Charlotte says, getting up and taking the bottle from Kallie. "Sit," she tells her and then looks at the blonde. "Olivia, honey, why don't you start at the beginning?" Charlotte then looks at me. "Can I get you something to drink? Some tea maybe?"

"He isn't going to be here long enough to drink anything," Kallie says, sitting down, and I see that she's wearing the same overalls she used to wear when we went riding. The same overalls I pulled down over her hips in the barn.

"Well, my ex-fiancé," Olivia starts to talk, and I look at her and try not to make my eyes go to Kallie, "was just charged with insider trading, and he stole a fuck ton of money from investors."

"Okay," I say, not seeing the issue. "Well, he stole from people he shouldn't steal from." She looks at me, wiggling her eyebrows.

"I always knew he was shady," Kallie says, and I avoid looking at her.

"Jesus," Casey says, grabbing the bottle from his mother and taking his own gulp. "Why didn't you tell us this?"

"How was I supposed to tell you guys this?" Kallie says. "Listen, they don't know anything about me."

"How can you be so stupid?" I say, and all eyes swing to

me. Casey looks like he's going to charge me, and Billy looks like he is going to shoot me in the foot, but still. "You live with her?" I ask her, and she avoids my eyes. "Mature," I mumble.

"You don't know me," Olivia says. "I'm Olivia."

"Nice to meet you," I say.

"Oh, I don't like you," she says, and I throw my hands up. "You aren't a nice person." Kallie sits beside her and laughs.

"They live together," Casey then says.

"So if you live together, chances are people know your name," I inform her. Kallie finally looks at me, and I see now it's starting to click. "And if they know who you are, then they will know everything about you."

I look at Billy and Casey. "If they know her name, they know where she grew up."

"Fuck," Casey says, "he's right."

"If they know where she is, they know where to find her." I shake my head. "I'm going to get eyes on the ground."

"She's safe if she's here," Casey says. "I have the whole farm wired."

"I'm going to get the boys to patrol the area more," I say. "The good news is nothing happens in this town without someone seeing."

"At least that works in our favor," Charlotte says.

"I'm going to set up a couple of things," I say. "I'll call you later."

"I'll be waiting," Casey says, and I nod, turning and walking out of the door. I'm almost to my truck when I hear the front door open and close. I don't know why I think it's Kallie, but I also don't know why I'm disappointed when I turn around and see Casey walking toward me.

"What now?" I say.

"This going to be a problem for you?" he asks, and I wait for him to say something else. "You are too close."

"I stopped caring when she cut me from her life," I say.

Opening the driver's door to my truck, I get in, starting it, and then look at him. "I have a job to do, and if I have to protect her, I will. Not because I care, but because it's my job."

"Good to know," he says and turns back and walks into the house. I pull out and feel eyes on my truck, but when I turn back, there is no one there.

Ten

KALLIE

The door closes, and I finally get up and go upstairs. My father calls my name, but I ignore him and slam my door. I don't want to do it, but I go to the window anyway, and I see him standing out there talking to Casey. I put my hand on my stomach and watch him get in the truck and leave. It's the same look he had eight years ago when he followed me home, and Casey sent him away.

But he didn't leave like he is now. No, instead he parked at the entrance of the farm and waited.

"You have to talk to him," my mother said when she walked into the room. I was standing there in the dress I had picked out for prom. A dress I had taken extra care in picking out because I wanted Jacob to be blown away.

"Mom, I can't," I said and turned to look at her, my heart broken in my chest. The tears poured out of me even though I wanted them to stop. I kicked off my boots and slid into my bed. He'd snuck into my room last night and held me all night long, so his smell was everywhere. I laid in the bed and pulled the covers over me, letting myself fall into the darkness with his smell all around me.

66

When I opened my eyes, I saw the sun coming in, but I didn't move. I only got up to go to the bathroom. I slipped out of my dress, tossing it into the trash bin in my room, then slipped into my pjs and let the darkness take me again over and over again. In my dreams, he told me it was going to be okay. In my dreams, I cried out from the pain I felt. In my dreams, I lost him over and over again. I'd wake with my pillow soaked with the tears I cried.

I heard whispers from the hallway, knowing it was my parents. I heard shouting, but my body didn't allow me to get up.

I felt the bed dip, and my heart sped up, thinking it was him. I opened my eyes, and it was my mother with her own tears running down her face. "You need to eat something."

"I can't," I whispered. "He's having a baby, Momma," I sobbed, the tears coming again. "He's having a baby."

"I know, pretty girl." She pushed back my hair.

"I can't stay here," I said between sobs. "I can't watch him have a family without me."

She only nodded and then got up and walked out of the room. When she came back, it was with a suitcase. I watched as she packed my stuff, and we made a plan to sneak out. "You have to hide in the back under a blanket."

"Why?" I asked her.

"He hasn't left the entrance in two days," my mother whispered. "I'll come to you in two days. Casey will stay with you until then."

I snuck out of my house in the middle of the night like a thief in the night. I cried the whole way as I prayed he'd follow us, but when we parked and Casey opened the door, I saw it was just us.

The knock on the door makes me look back, and I come back to the here and now. "Yeah," I say. The door opens, and it's my mother.

"You have to come down and eat something please." She

begs me just as she did eight years ago. "We have to talk things out."

"I will," I say, and she walks to me and hugs me.

"Nothing is going to touch you here," she says, and I breathe in her smell.

"Kallie!" Casey shouts my name up the stairs. "Get your ass back down here."

"Well, then," my mother says, trying not to laugh, and I shake my head.

"I should have finished the whole bottle of whiskey," I mumble. When we walk back down, I see that Olivia is sitting on the couch with her feet tucked under her, and she is holding a teacup.

"Your father just handed me tea with whiskey," she says, and she takes a small sip. "I could get used to this Southern thing."

"Family meeting," my father says, and I just look at him. "Kitchen."

Olivia gets up. Walking to the kitchen, I look back and see that Casey has his hand on her shoulder, and he walks to the kitchen with her.

I sit on one of the chairs, and Casey sits next to Olivia. "We need to tell the boys what we are dealing with in case they see anything," my father starts to say, and Casey nods his head.

"Already on it," he starts. "I think Olivia should stay with me."

"What?" Olivia whispers, and I groan.

"Just hear me out, darlin'," he says. "Separating you two is the smart thing to do. If they want to get to you."

"He's right," Olivia says. "It's my fault that this is coming to your parents' home. I couldn't live with myself if something happened to you and your parents."

"Olivia, I knew the risks when I packed my bag and brought you here. This is not your fault," I say.

"I mean, in some ways it is. I should have just never come here," Olivia says softly and looks at my parents. "I'm so sorry."

"This isn't your fault," my mother says, and my father smiles at her.

"Family takes care of family," my father says, and I lean over the table and put my hand on hers.

"Sister from another mister," I joke with her, then look at Casey. "You can't sleep with her. She's your sister."

"She is not even close to being my sister," Casey says, shaking his head.

"Kallie," my father says, and I look at him. "I get why you are angry." I sit up now. "But you have to let Jacob do his job."

"I'm not getting in his way. I want to stay out of his way. I want to be so far away from him that I moved to the other side of the country. If I could, I would even go farther." I slap the table. "I want nothing to do with him. Not one thing. I don't want to see him. I don't want to talk about him. I don't want to even hear his name."

"Honey," my mother says, and I look at her. "He lives here, and he is pretty much all over town." She looks down. "Ethan, too." I look at her confused. "His son."

I push away from the table. "I need some air," I tell them and walk out of the house and straight to the barn. Walking through the grass, I spot a couple of the boys who smile at me and hold up their cowboy hats to say hello. I walk into the stalls and see Ricardo, who has been with my family since my father took over the farm. "There she is," he says, coming to me. He's in his usual uniform of Levi's, a button-down checkered shirt, and cowboy boots. He opens his arms for me, and I hug him. "Was wondering when you'd come back."

"Well, here I am." I step out of his hug and look around. "I'm going to take my girl out."

"She's already saddled for you." I smile at him as he walks over to her stall and brings her out for me.

"Hey, my girl," I say softly to her and nuzzle her neck. Climbing on the saddle, I say, "I'll put her away when I get back."

I gallop out into the field, and when I'm in the clearing, I push her fast. I feel the wind on my face as my hair whips back. I don't even steer her; I just let her be free. It's only when she slows down do I see she is taking me right back to where I was last night. I get off her and lead her to the water. I'm not here for more than a minute before I hear the sounds of twigs snapping, and I straighten my back up and my heart speeds up just a bit. *Maybe coming all this way without anyone was a stupid idea.*

I wonder if Casey has it wired all the way out here. I look around to see where I could escape. My hands get clammy, and I turn to jump back on the horse when I see him walking out of the woods. As I watch him walking with his head down, I take him in. His shoulders are wider, his arms much bigger, and I see a little bit of ink coming up out of his collar. I wonder when he got that, and I wonder why he got it. I shake my head and look around to see if I can get away without him seeing me, but then he looks up and sees me, and he stops in his tracks.

"What are you doing here?" he asks, and I look around.

"Are you asking me what I'm doing here, on my property?" I want him to take off his hat to see if his hair is still black and long on top. I wonder if it still feels silky. I remember when he didn't cut it for a year because I loved to play with it. He shakes his head. "What are you doing here is the question."

"I came to see the size of the rock," he says and walks to the rock. "I'll have it gone by tomorrow."

"Good," I say. He stands there, and I turn to look back at the water, ignoring the pull to him.

"You shouldn't be out here alone," he says, and I want to yell at him and ask why he even cares. I want to yell that what I do has nothing to do with him. I want to yell that he needs to go and take care of his wife and their child.

"You should be at home with your wife and child and not worry about where I am." My mouth opens before I can take the words back. The last thing I want him to know is that I care or that I even think of him.

He ignores my outburst. "I'm going to have a meeting with the guys tomorrow, and I would like for you and Olivia to be there." He takes off his hat and scratches his head. "It's good to have everyone working with each other."

I nod at him, swallowing over the lump in my throat as I look at him. The man I wanted to share everything with; the man I wanted to have children with; the man who said he would hold my hand forever. The same man who holds his wife at night and then tucks their child into bed. Maybe coming home wasn't a good idea. I thought I could handle it. Thought it would be fine. I. Was. Wrong. Nothing about being here is fine.

"I'll text Casey about it," he says, looking down. I know he wants to say something else, but he doesn't. "See you tomorrow." He turns and walks away from me. This time, I watch his back until I can't see him anymore. Only when I feel wetness on my hand do I realize I'm crying. Only then do I fall to my knees and bury my face in my hands. I cry for the boy I lost, I cry for the love I lost, and I cry for the piece of me I lost.

I'm raw, and my whole body aches from head to toe. I get back on the horse and take my time getting home. The sun is setting, and when I get to the barn, Ricardo is sitting at the desk. "Welcome back," he says, and I smile at him. I wonder how awful I look. I'm sure he can tell I've been crying. "I'll take her."

"Thank you," I say. After handing him the reins, I walk

back to the house. Olivia is lying on the swing outside. She's slipped out of her jeans and is now in yoga pants and a T-shirt. "Hey," I say, climbing up the steps to the porch and sitting on the end of the swing.

"I can't believe this is happening," she says softly, her eyes staring straight ahead. "He's taken everything from me." I don't say anything as I swing with her. "And now I've put your family in harm's way."

"Meh." I shrug. "We can take care of ourselves."

She turns and looks at me, and her eyelashes are wet from tears. "You guys don't deserve this."

"Neither do you," I remind her. "It'll all get settled soon. When is he going to court?"

"Two weeks," she tells me. "And I have to go."

"We will," I say. "It's me and you." I look ahead.

"How're you feeling?" she asks, and I look at her.

"Like I'm empty," I say. "There is nothing left inside me. I have nothing else to give. I have nothing that anyone wants."

"Then he's stupid," she says softly and turns back to stare at the horizon. "He sure is pretty, though." I don't respond. Instead, I just look out at the horizon with her, and when my mother comes out to call us in for dinner, we just look at each other.

"Will you come with me to Casey's house?" she asks. "Not to sleep. You should sleep here. They are right about that. But to work and stuff."

"Yes," I say, and she grabs my hand. We walk into the house, and we stop when we see Casey standing there with his feet spread apart and his arms crossed over his chest.

"What now?" I ask, and he just looks at me.

"Did you forget to mention something?" He looks at me, and I wait as my heart beats in my chest. "You spoke to Jacob." My mother drops the cup she has in her hand, and it shatters on the floor.

All eyes turn to her, and I shake my head. Her hands shake, and she walks over to the chair and sits down. "I just need a minute." My father rushes to her side. Squatting down in front of her, he grabs her hands in his and kisses them. "I'm fine."

"You are running yourself to the ground," he says, and she looks at him. She takes one of her hands and cups his cheek. "I can't do this without you."

"That's so romantic," Olivia says and then looks at me. "I need me a Southern man."

I try not to laugh as I look over at Casey. "I think you already got one."

Eleven

JACOB

I know I should just go get Ethan and go home. I know I should turn back and go to the rock. I know deep in my bones it's a bad idea. My head is spinning. I don't know what the fuck she did or how she did it, but she is in danger, and she is fighting me.

I make my way to the rock that Casey wants off his property, walking with my head down. My head is bringing me back to when I used to walk with her by my side. Her hand was always in mine, even if it was just her pinky. The sounds of the stream fill the silence of the day with some birds chirping. I'm not expecting anyone to be here, least of all her. And she's all alone after we just had the conversation that someone is after her.

The minute I ask her a question, I see her sass come out, and I almost want to smile. I want to ask her to sit on the rock with me. I want to know what she has been up to. I want to know if she found someone to love her.

"You should be at home with your wife and child and not worry about where I am." The minute she says that, I want to take a step back. I want to tell her that I don't have a wife, that

I would never take a wife who wasn't her. How does she not know that I'm not married? How did no one tell her that I never was with Savannah especially after she left?

I walk away from her, wanting to take her in my arms and see if her kisses are the same. To see if she melts in my arms the same way, to see if the kiss is just as good as I remember. Is it as good as in my dreams? I get in my truck and call Casey. I expect him to send me to voice mail, but he answers right away.

"What part of she might be in danger does she not understand?" I say, not even bothering to say hello.

"What the heck are you talking about?" he asks.

"I just found Kallie by herself at the creek," I say. "I could have been anyone."

"I'll take care of it," he says. "It won't happen again."

"Tomorrow morning at ten a.m., my office. It's time to get a game plan going to make sure no one gets injured in the crossfire."

"This doesn't change anything," Casey says, and he hangs up. I toss my phone to the side and make my way to my mother's house.

"There he is," my mother says. I watch as Ethan gets up and runs to me.

"Dad," he says, jumping into my arms, "you took forever."

"Sorry, kiddo," I say, leaning and kissing his neck. I'm about to ask him about his day when the front door opens, and Savannah walks in wearing white jeans and a tank top. Her black hair is curled like normal.

"There they are," she says with a smile and comes over to us. "How was your day?" she asks Ethan, leaning and kissing his neck.

I put him down, and he runs back to the kitchen. "Mom is here, Grandma."

"I didn't know you were going to be here?" I say, and it's

almost as if I step away from her in case someone is watching, which is ridiculous.

"Yeah, your mom called and thought it would be good to drop by for dinner," she says. Looking in the kitchen, she then turns to me. "I heard about the grocery store."

"Shocking," I say, shaking my head. "It's only been three hours." Taking off the hat on my head, I toss it on the coffee table and go sit on the couch.

"How bad was it?" she asks, and I just shake my head.

"She thinks we're married," I say, and she takes a step back. "I know. That's what I thought, too."

"Why would she think we're married?" she asks, sitting down on the couch and facing me. "Who told her that?"

"I haven't spoken or seen her in eight years, so I have no idea why she would think or say that."

"It's safe to say every person knows that I've had a child out of wedlock," Savannah says, laughing. "I almost had the 'A' tattooed on my chest to make sure if you didn't know, you know now."

"I don't know." I pull my hair on the top of my head. I keep it longer than I did when she left. I want to say it's because it's easier to style, but the fact is, she loved my hair long.

I look at Savannah, and I'm brought back to the day I went to see her.

I knocked on her door. I wanted to pound on it and break it down, but she answered right away. Her face was pale, her eyes almost sunken in, and her lips were white. "What's wrong?"

"I have morning sickness," she said and turned to walk back into her little apartment. She was the only eighteen-year-old I knew living on her own. Her mother took off as soon as everyone found out she was pregnant.

I closed the door behind me, and she sat on her worn couch. "I'm so sorry, Jacob."

"Whose is it?" I asked, not moving from the door.

She looked down and then looked up at me. "Liam's." She said his name, and I just looked at her. "Don't even go there. I know. I know. He's a horrible person."

"How the fuck did that ever happen?" I asked her, and she sobbed.

"He said he loved me," she said, and I wanted to tell her that he didn't love anyone but himself. "You can't tell Beau."

"Jesus fucking Christ," I finally shouted at her, "do you know what you've done?" I know I shouldn't lash out at her, but I do anyway.

"Um, hello." I hear Savannah, and I blink when the front door opens, and I look over to see Beau coming in.

He sees us both sitting here. He looks at me and then at Savannah, and I'm wondering how the fuck she can't see that he's in love with her. I swear he walks around with hearts in his eyes when she's around. The smile on her face is even bigger than it was when I walked into the room when he walks to her and bends down in front of her.

"Hey, there." He kisses her cheek, and I swear if she sighs, I'm going to throw up.

"Dinner is ready," Ethan says, and I get up. "Hey, Uncle Beau," he says, walking to him, and they high-five each other. Well, at least out of all the lies Savannah has told, calling him Uncle is the truth.

Savannah gets up and goes into the kitchen and helps set the table. Beau's eyes follow her the whole time, and he turns. "I heard something."

"I can imagine," I say, getting up.

"Did you really tell her to go to hell?" he asks me quietly, and I look over at him.

"What are you talking about?" I ask.

"Word on the street is you saw her in the grocery store and told her to go to hell and get out of your town," he says, looking down. I just stand here in shock. "I take it that some-where along the line, the story changed."

"A lot," I say and go into the kitchen. I sit at the table and eat, and we don't bring up Kallie. Ethan tells us all about his day, and he goes on and on about the sleepover he has on Saturday for his friend's birthday party.

When we leave my mother's, Ethan asks to sleep over at her house, and I don't fight it and neither does Savannah since she has to work. "Are you coming in tonight?" she asks Beau, and he shakes his head.

"I have a big meeting tomorrow morning," he says and goes to his car. "Have a good night." We both watch him walk to his BMW, and he gets in and takes off.

"If you sigh, I will throw up," I say, and she shakes her head.

"I don't sigh." She pushes my shoulder and walks away from me. "I'll get him from school tomorrow."

Shaking my head, I get in my truck. I should just head home, but I don't. I head back over to Kallie's to do a wellness check. I pull up and see the light on in her room. I spot a couple of my guys and wave at them and then head home.

The night pretty much consists of me tossing and turning. Finally, the last time I check the clock, it's three a.m. When my phone rings at eight, I jump out of bed. "McIntyre."

"Hey, it's Monica."

"Yeah," I grumble out.

"Just confirming that you have a meeting at ten with the squad," she says.

"Yeah. I'll be there," I say and toss the phone on the bed. By the time I shower and pour my coffee and get into the car, I'm already late. I rushed and just put on my black jeans with my white shirt. I left the hat off today, pushing my hair back with my hand. I slip on my aviator glasses when I start my car, and when I pull up to the station, I see that Casey's truck is already here. Walking up the steps, I open the glass door and try not to stumble back. She's standing there with tight white jeans molding her every curve. She's wearing a short-sleeve gray silk shirt, and it's tucked in the front and is loose over her breasts. I don't take off my glasses as I spot the highest heeled shoes I've ever seen.

"About time you showed up," Casey says, and she finally looks at me. I want to smile and say hi. I want to walk up to her and push her hair away from her face and kiss her.

"I'm on time," I say and then look at Monica. "Morning."

"Morning yourself," she says, smiling and leaning back in her chair.

"The guys here?" I ask, and she nods her head.

"Already in the back," she says. "Do you want me to get you a coffee?"

"Well, then," Olivia finally says, turning to Casey, "do all the women flirt with married men in the South?"

Casey watches her, and Kallie looks down. "Wait a second," Monica says, "he's not married." She points at me, and I swear Kallie got whiplash with how fast her head flew up. "The answer to that is no."

Olivia stares at us dumbfounded. "Well, that is very good to know." She nods and then looks at Casey. "Awkward." He shakes his head.

"Let's get this thing started," I say and walk past them to the back. The sound of the girls' heels are clicking on the floor, and when we get into the room with my squad, the guys sit there with their mouths hanging open.

"Gentlemen," Casey says. Looking around the room, I see that no one was here when the shit went down with me and Kallie. They are all a year younger than me.

"Grady," I say, and he gets up and smiles at Olivia and then bigger at Kallie. I suddenly want to throat punch him. "Meet Olivia and Kallie." Grady's smile fades as the name clicks into place. "Ladies, have a seat." The girls go to the chairs, and Kallie stops when she spots the picture of Ethan and me. Her eyes fill with tears, but she blinks them away and sits down. When all seats are taken, the only one left is right beside Kallie. I pull it out and sit down, taking off my glasses. "Shall we start?"

Twelve

KALLIE

"Shall we start?" He sits beside me, and my body goes on full alert. I could lie and say that I didn't take my time getting ready today. The white jeans are my favorite pair, and I know that I look awesome in them. The same for the shirt. The shoes? Well, the shoes speak for themselves. Will my feet burn in an hour? Yes. Did I have to walk barefoot to the truck killing my feet on the rocks? Yes.

But a girl has to do what a girl has to do, and apparently, it hurts doing it.

I thought I was ready to face him. I thought it wouldn't bother me. It did. Watching him walk in wearing black jeans that show off just how big his thighs got made my stomach flip. His shirt again pulled across his chest, and I was looking for the ink that I saw pieces of yesterday. His hair is longer than I thought it was. You can see where he pushed it back with his fingers. Or maybe Savannah did it when he got out of the shower when she kissed him goodbye. The thought makes me want to throw up. I put my hand on my stomach, expecting it to come up. I was so in my head I didn't know what was going on until she said the words that made my head snap up. "He's not married."

What does that mean? Why? It made no sense. Jacob would never not marry the mother of his child. We had a fight once when I asked him about it. The memory comes to me like it was yesterday.

"What do you mean we have to get married?" I asked him as we lay in my bed.

"If you are pregnant with my child." He looked at me, getting up and grabbing his shirt. "It's a given you are going to be my wife."

"Why does it have to be a given, Jacob?" I asked, getting on my elbows.

"I don't make the rules, baby," he said softly and leaned down, kissing me tenderly. "I just follow them."

"That's barbaric." I put my hand on his cheek. "I wouldn't marry you."

He smirked like he always did. Sometimes his dimple came out, and this was one of those times. "Lies." He turned and slammed out of the room.

"I think we should start at the beginning," Grady says, opening his notepad and leaning back in his chair.

I look over at Olivia whose hands start to shake. Casey leans over and grabs one in his, bringing it to his lips. I see everyone at the table look at each other.

"I don't even know where to start," Olivia says, her voice shaking just a bit. "Bottom line, I was dating a guy. We got engaged, and it was great, and then it was not so great." I listen as she tells her side of the story, my own hands in my lap. "The detective called me."

"Kallie." I hear my name and look over at Grady. "Are you single?"

I'm about to smile at him when Jacob snaps, "What the fuck does that have to do with any of this?" I don't look over at him, but I see him in my side view. His jaw gets tight while Olivia snickers beside me.

"Well, for one, we have to eliminate that it isn't her boyfriend looking for her," Grady says, tapping his finger on the table.

"I'm single," I say. "We can eliminate me from this."

"Good to know," Grady says and smiles shyly at me.

"Well, if we're finished with the dating game," Jacob says, and I still don't look over at him. "Olivia, do you know how many people we are talking about?"

"The last count was eighty-nine people," she says, and she shakes her head. "I had no idea that he used their money for his lifestyle."

"I am going to reach out to the detective on the case," Jacob says, and the guys around the table nod. None of them really says anything, and if I can say, they all look like badasses. Each one of them is muscled, wearing a white T-shirt, and I have to wonder if maybe it's the uniform. They actually look like they can do calendars. "I want all eyes open," Jacob says. "I also want one car parked at the Barnes' residence overnight. We will have a rotation," he says, and I wonder if he will be there one night. "Other than that, we should be on the lookout for anyone we don't know coming through town."

"That should be easy," one of the guys says, laughing, "especially with summer coming."

"It'll be hard, but we can have a couple of feelers out. I'm going to touch base with the fire commander also," Jacob says. "I'll have more tomorrow." When the guys all get up, I assume the meeting is over, so I move to get up. I put my hand down on the table, and our hands touch. Even though I snatch my hand back as fast as I can, I can't stop the tingle that remains from his touch.

"Before you guys go," Jacob says, "I want to see you in my

office." He looks over at Casey and Grady. "Grady, can you join us?"

"Are you okay?" I ask Olivia, who nods her head.

"I could ask you the same," she mumbles. We walk out of the office, and I wait for Casey to walk in front of us into Jacob's office. I look around and spot a picture of his father's official portrait on the wall with the recommendations he got when he was sheriff. Beside him is a picture of Jacob smiling.

I cross my arms over my chest, and my eyes find the picture behind his desk. His arm is wrapped around Savannah with their son in front of him. I try not to let it hurt. The perfect smiles on the faces of his perfect family. "Excuse me," I say, "I need the restroom."

"I'll take her," Grady says, and I look at Olivia, who looks at me, knowing I saw the picture. "This way," he says, putting his hand on my lower back and ushering me to the bathroom at the end of the hall.

"Thank you." Looking at him, I know I should find him hot. He is hot—blond hair, blue eyes, nice body—but it's just like all the others. Nothing makes my heart flutter.

"I'll wait for you here," he says, and I just smile at him. I enter the bathroom and close the door. My head falls on the cold door as the tears escape my eyes. I close my eyes and let the tears fall down my cheeks.

"One of these days, it won't hurt," I whisper to myself. "One of these days." Turning, I walk over to the sink and turn on the cold water. Wetting one of the brown paper towels that they have, I dab at my cheeks. I try to make myself presentable, but it's obvious I was crying. Tossing the paper in the garbage, I take a deep breath and open the door, and Grady turns to face me from the middle of the room. His phone is in his hand, and he looks at me.

"Are you okay?" he asks softly, coming to stand in front of me.

"Yeah," I say, looking down and trying to think of something that isn't as depressing as pining after the man who broke your heart and had a family with someone else.

He puts his hand on my arm. "It's going to be okay, Kallie." I look up and smile at him. "I promise that nothing will happen to you."

I'm about to thank him for being kind. "Grady, you think you can join us in a meeting?" Jacob says from the doorway, and I look over at him. He stands there, and I want him to look horrible, but he doesn't.

"I was waiting for Kallie," Grady says. "We're coming now."

We walk back into the office, and I ignore the leers coming from Jacob. I also ignore looking at anything but my feet. I don't know what is discussed. I can't even tell you anything. The only thing I know is that the longer I stay in this room, the more I feel my skin crawling. "Let's get out of here." I hear Casey, and I'm the first one to turn and walk out of the room but not before I spot one more photograph.

It looks like it was taken right when his son was born. He has tears in his eyes as he holds the little pink baby in his arms swaddled in a white cover with his father beside him. I walk out of the room, and it's almost as if something is choking me. "I can't breathe." I look over at Olivia, who looks frantic. "I just can't," I say, trying to catch my breath, but nothing is helping.

I count to ten and not even that helps. I stop halfway to the door, and I have to bend over. "What's happening?" Grady asks.

"She's having a panic attack," Olivia hisses and comes over to me. "Just take in small breaths," she says, rubbing my back, but I'm struggling even with that. My heart just races even more, and my hands start to tingle, which only means I'm going to go down soon.

"Chair," I say between trying to get my heart to settle. I'm suddenly lifted in the air, and I think it's Casey, but it's not.

"Get a cold rag!" Jacob shouts, and I want to push away from him when he leads me to a chair in a common room. He sits me down and squats down in front of me. "You need breathe in through your nose and out through your mouth."

"I think she knows how to breathe," Casey hisses.

Olivia joins Jacob in front of me. "The beach," she says, and I look at her. "Remember when we went to the beach, and I got a sunburn?" I try to smile, and my heart slows down. While Monica runs over with a rag and hands it to Jacob, who moves my hair to the side and puts it on my neck. "You told me to wear sunscreen." Olivia tells the story. "I said I don't need sunscreen, I'm from LA." I shake my head now as my breathing finally returns to normal.

"You burned like a lobster," I finish for her. I close my eyes, and my heart starts to slow down.

"She's good," Olivia says. I open my eyes, and all I can see is Jacob with worry all over his face. But I close my eyes again and just lean back in the chair, waiting a bit longer before trying to get up.

"How many attacks does she get?" Jacob asks Olivia.

"It doesn't matter," she tells him, and he is about to ask another question when I open my eyes.

"I'm good," I say, taking the rag off my neck and handing it back to Jacob. "Thank you," I say softly and look over at Casey who pushes his way to me and holds out his hand. I take it and stand, not once letting his hand go.

"We should get some food in you," Casey says. When I nod, he leads me out, and I don't make eye contact with anyone. "What the fuck just happened?" he hisses when we are standing by his truck.

"She had a panic attack," Olivia says for me, "and it

doesn't help to be yelled at, cowboy." She puts her hands on her hips. "Calm voices."

He looks at her, and he smiles. "That so, darlin'?" His voice goes soft, and I swear she sighs.

"You two are gross," I say, looking around. "You know what I want?" They both look at me. "I want a root beer float."

"Do you know how much sugar is in that?" Olivia asks in shock, and I look at her. She wore her pink pants today with a small gold belt, her white shirt just short of the top of the pants, showing just a touch of her skin. Her nude Louboutins finish the outfit perfectly.

"Enough that I might get two." I wink at her and turn around. "Casey, let's go to the diner." He nods at me, and he walks in the middle of us.

He pulls open the door, making the bell ring. I step in, and the chatter stops. "Well, then," Olivia says, and I look around at the diner that we used to go to after school every single Friday. Most of us were having the 'Friday Night Special' right before the big football game.

"Well, I'll be damned." Mr. Lewis comes out of the back in his usual brown pants and white shirt. His white apron is folded and tied around his waist. His white hat is on his head. "If it isn't Miss Kallie."

"In the flesh," I say to him, and he smiles. "How've you been?"

"Never better," he says. "You grab a seat, and I'll send out Delores."

I walk over to an empty table in the middle of the room. "Are those jukeboxes?" Olivia asks, pointing at one of the booths with the classic jukeboxes on the table.

"Yeah," Casey says, holding the chair for her to sit in. "Some work and some don't."

"That is so cool," she says, looking around at the old pictures that line the wall.

When Delores comes over, I order a root beer float and a cheeseburger with the works. Olivia looks at the menu, asking for the same and then looks at me. "There is no salad on that menu."

"I think there is a piece of lettuce in the burger," I say, throwing my head back and laughing. When the door opens and the bell rings, my heart stops in my chest.

"You did not." I hear Beau say when Savannah laughs and looks over her shoulder at Jacob who just smiles at her walking in.

"This should be interesting," Olivia says from beside me, but she isn't the only one thinking that.

Thirteen

JACOB

The door closes behind them, and I think it's only then that I breathe for the first time since I walked in.

I tried to keep my cool in the meeting, tried to ignore that she was so close to me. When Grady asked her if she was dating anyone, I wanted to slam my hand on the table. The meeting in my office didn't go any better when she stepped out with him. I counted to seven hundred, and he wasn't back yet, so I made an excuse of needing water. I wasn't ready to catch him with his hand on her arm. I wanted to rip his arm out of his socket.

I kept my calm, but when she walked out of the room and had a panic attack in front of me, I snapped. I lost my cool, and I did everything I shouldn't do like take her in my arms and hold her without thinking or telling myself not to. Having her in my arms shifted things in me. I set her down and want to hold her hand, but instead, I watch Olivia talk to her. My chest feels like it's being crushed seeing her hurt. I shouldn't fucking care, yet nothing will stop it. I've loved her my whole life. I still love her.

I watch her walk out of the office with Casey, making sure

she is okay. I stand here with my eyes on her. Grady is next to me, and Monica is next to Grady. "Well, that settles that," Grady finally says, and I look down at the floor and rub the back of my neck with my hand.

"It really does," Monica says, shaking her head. "It really sucks she's pretty."

Grady laughs and looks at her. "She is fucking beautiful."

"That's enough!" I yell at them, my head feeling like it's going to fucking explode. The front door opens, and Beau and Savannah come in.

"There he is," Savannah says. "Beau is paying for lunch."

"Why?" I ask, and she shakes her head. "He bet yet again and lost." She looks at him.

He reaches out and pulls her in and kisses the top of her head. "You're a pain in my ass." She doesn't move out of his touch. "Always have been."

"Always will be." She puts an arm around his waist, looking at me. "Now get your radio."

"I'm not on duty," I inform her and then look at Grady. "I'll call you later, and we can go over everything."

"Looking forward to it," he says and turns to go back to his office.

Turning to Monica, I say, "Call me if there is anything."

"Will do, boss." She nods, and I walk out of the station.

The three of us walk to the diner. "So what did you bet this time?"

"It's stupid," Beau says, and Savannah claps her hands in front of her.

"It was so good," Savannah says. "Mrs. Hoover was out at the bar last night." She starts with the nickname we gave to our old principal. Word is she liked to suck cock. Or at least, that is the rumor. "I bet him that she would make a play for him."

"Oh my God," I say, putting my hand to my stomach. "Isn't she like seventy?"

"I swear I heard her tell a couple of the men that she would love to have him leave his boots under her bed," Savannah teases him as he pulls open the door to the diner.

"You did not," Beau says to her over his shoulder.

Savannah laughs and looks over her shoulder at me. "I did, too." I smile and shake my head. There's never a dull moment with these two. I suddenly bump into Savannah in front of me as I see everyone stare at us. It takes a moment, and I finally see why. There in the middle of the diner is Kallie.

"Oh my God," Beau says, leaving Savannah and me at the door and going over to her. "Look at you," he says, smiling. She gets up for him and smiles. He wraps his arms around her and even picks her up. "I heard you were back in town."

"Are you going to be okay?" Savannah asks, and I don't look at her. I try to talk myself into not killing my best friend.

Casey looks at me and just glares and shakes his head as if I planned this. As if I knew she would be here. "I'm not hungry anymore," Savannah says.

"We are all adults," I say, and she looks at me with tears in her eyes. "We can eat in the same place."

"Easy for you to say," she mumbles. "You didn't have the baby of the man she loves."

"Loved." I correct her and usher her to one of the booths as we wait for Beau to return.

We both pretend to read the menu. "Well, that wasn't as bad as I thought it would be," Beau says, sitting next to Savannah. "You okay?" he asks, and she shakes her head and wipes away a tear.

My leg moves up and down with nerves. I want to go up to her and make sure she's okay. I want her to know that I care. I want her to know that I didn't fucking sleep with Savannah. I want to tell her all my secrets. My stomach falls when I look over and see her getting up and wiping away a tear. She smiles and pretends to be okay, but I know she isn't. She picks up her to-go drink, and they walk out the door. I watch Olivia put her arm around Kallie and walk her to the truck.

"I'm not hungry," I tell the table. "Rain check."

"Yeah, of course," Beau says, and I get up. "I'll call you later."

"Yeah," I say and walk out of the diner toward my truck. I sit in the driver's seat and put the key inside. My head throbs as my chest feels crushed, so I go to the only place that calms me. I park the truck in my secret spot and make my way down to the creek. The place that calms me yet breaks me equally.

My mind feels like it's going to explode with all the memories rushing back. All the memories—good, bad, sad, ugly—replay in my head like a movie.

The first time I kissed her. Her telling me that she loved me the first time. The first time I made love to her. The first time we got into a fight and she threw me out of her house. The first time I came crawling back. The first time she woke up in my arms. The last time I kissed her, right before our world got taken from us. The last time I saw her here was with tears streaming down her face.

I'm almost at the creek when I spot him. Someone who is definitely not from here. He stands with his jeans and leather jacket on as he takes pictures. I watch him for a bit, and then he takes out his phone and does something on it. I take out my own phone and snap a picture of him.

As I step out into the clearing, the branches snap under my feet, getting the guy's attention. His black hair is pushed all the way back, his eyes in surprise that someone should be here. "Can I help you?" I ask, and he changes now.

He laughs nervously. "Not really. I think I'm lost. I was ..." He turns around and pretends to be looking at something. "On a hike and I must have taken the wrong turn."

"Yeah, those trails are tricky." I play into his story even though there are no fucking trails anywhere in this town. "You should really have brought a guide with you."

"Yeah, I should have," he says, looking down at his feet, and I notice he's wearing Chucks.

"Where you from?" I ask, trying to reel him in.

"Oh, I'm a West Coast boy," he says. "Figured I'd get away to clear my head."

"Well, you came to the right place," I say, "but this is private property."

"Really?" He acts shocked. "I didn't know."

I shrug. "Let me help you to your car," I say, and he nods at me.

"Do you remember where you parked?"

"I think a little over that way." He points to the path that leads to the road.

"Well, let me escort you there." I hold out my hand and wait for him to walk in front of me.

"You really don't have to do that," he says, looking over his shoulder at me.

"It's my pleasure." I smile tight, and I take him to his car that is parked on the side of the road. I make a mental note of his license place, but I have no doubt it's a rental.

"Well, thank you," he says, unlocking his car door. "People in the South are so trusting."

"That's what we make you believe," I say. "People in the South also shoot first and ask questions later."

He laughs nervously, getting into his car. "I didn't get your name."

"You didn't," I say. "I didn't get yours either."

"Dwayne," he says.

"Nice to meet you, Dwayne. You have a safe journey home." I turn and walk back to the creek, stopping and turning to see which way he drives. When I see him pull off, I run to my truck, getting in and calling Monica.

"I need you to run this plate," I say, shouting off the number.

"I'll call you when I get the information," she says. I hang up and call the one man I have spent the past eight years avoiding.

"What now?" he answers.

"Five minutes, your parents' house." I don't even wait for him to respond before I toss my phone on the passenger seat. Pulling up to Kallie's house, I stop the truck and grab my phone. I look around to see if I see anything when I walk to the door. I don't have to knock when the door swings open and a pissed-off Casey is there. He walks out and closes the door behind him.

"She's been home two days. Two and every single time she turns around she's hit with the reality that you fucked another woman," he says between clenched teeth. "I had to fucking carry her in today." He looks around. "After having a panic attack where she almost fucking fainted."

"You think I want to cause her pain?" I now stand up to him. "You think that in any of this, I want her to feel the pain that I feel every fucking day?" I shake my head. "This isn't about me. I found someone creeping around the creek."

He steps back at my words. "What did you just say?" His jaw clenches. "Let's go inside."

He walks back inside. "Mom, Dad!" he yells, then yells up the stairs, "Kallie, Darlin'!"

"What is all this screaming going on?" Charlotte comes out of the kitchen, and she's wiping her hands on a towel, and you can see she was crying. "Jacob, honey, I don't think ..."

"Mom, not now." Casey goes to the liquor cabinet. "Mom, please go get the girls," he says, taking a swig. He goes to hand me the bottle, but he just shrugs when I shake my head. "Suit yourself."

Charlotte comes down with Olivia right behind her who glares at me. "I don't like you," she says, and I almost roll my eyes.

"Um ..." Charlotte says. "Kallie will be down in a minute."

"What is all this about?" Billy says, coming into the house from the backyard.

"We are waiting for Kallie," Casey says, taking another swig.

"What is up with you?" Olivia gets close to Casey, and he just shakes his head. I hear her coming down the stairs. Her hair is piled on top of her head. She wears pink shorts and a white shirt, and she avoids looking at me.

"Everyone's here," Casey says. "You can start anytime you want."

"After I left the diner, I went to the creek," I start, and my eyes are on Kallie. She looks down at the floor, and I see her wipe a tear away. "I just needed to clear my head." She shakes her head. "I was walking there, and I saw a guy. Knew right away he was not where he was supposed to be. He was taking pictures," I say, and now she looks up at me with her mouth open. "He claims he got lost on the trails."

"There are no trails," Billy says, looking at Casey who takes another swig.

"I got his picture," I tell them and open my phone. "He said his name is Dwayne." I hand the phone to Olivia, who shakes her head, then passes the phone to Kallie, who takes it in her hand and shakes her head also.

"I walked him to his car and got his plate number," I say. "I'm running the plate, but I'm not expecting it to be that easy."

"You are not allowed at that creek," Casey says to Kallie.

"You don't have to worry about that. After today, I think

it's safe to say I'm going into hibernation," she says, getting up. "I'm not feeling well."

"I'll go with her," Olivia says, and then looks at Casey. "Enough of the drinking please."

Casey does not do what he's told. He does not listen to anyone but his mother, and that is only on occasion. I'm waiting for him to laugh at her and take another gulp. Instead, he nods at her and puts the bottle down, and I'm not the only one with their mouth hanging open. Olivia looks at him and gives him a shy smile, and she walks upstairs just as my phone rings.

"Hello?" I say, looking at Casey when I hear Grady. "I'm with Casey. I'm going to put you on speaker."

"Okay, so the plate you got is from a rental agency," he says, and I shake my head.

"I knew it," I say.

"But get this, when I called the rental agency, they said that this car was not rented out. So the guy goes to check, and the plate was stolen off the car," Grady says. "We have two of the guys going over there to check the surveillance footage. I'll keep you posted."

"Thank you," I say and hang up.

"What in the fuck is going on?" Billy says.

"I have no idea," I say and look upstairs, "but whatever it is, those two should never be alone." I want to go up and check on her. I want to make sure she is okay. Instead, I turn around and head for the front door. "I'll be in touch," I say right before I slam the door behind me.

Fourteen

KALLIE

"Four days." I hear moaned from beside me while I answer my last email from work. "It's been four days and nothing."

I look over my laptop at her. "I don't even know what you are talking about." I grab my cup of coffee and take a sip. I'm sitting at Casey's kitchen table while we work. We have been alternating working from my parents' and Casey's.

"One, it's been four days since we've been outside." As she starts talking, she gets up to go to the fridge and takes out the bottle of white wine that I know she put in there. I look over her shoulder at the clock. It's just a bit after noon.

"We were outside yesterday." I smile at her, and she glares at me as she stands at the island. "Okay, fine, walking to my parents' house and then sitting on the back porch is not being outside."

"Thank you," she says, drinking more wine and then taking a big gulp. "It's also been four days since Casey kissed me."

I close my eyes tight. "Eww."

"I know, I know," she says, sitting at the table now with

the bottle of wine in one hand and the glass in the other, "but there is literally no one else to talk to about this." I look at her. "I have you and your mother." I put my hand in front of my mouth. "I don't think it's a good idea to be like I want to bone your son."

"You shouldn't say that to anyone," I say, and she shakes her head.

"This is crazy," she says. "I'm living in his house. I sleep under his roof."

"Okay," I say, confused.

"I just ..." She looks down. "What does he even do?"

I swallow down, and I think about what to tell her. "He does a little bit of everything." I mean, technically it's the truth. He does do a little bit of everything. I wait for her to ask me what in the hell that means, but she doesn't.

Olivia looks at me, pinching her eyebrows together. "We are living together and nothing. It's just," she says, shaking her head, "I just, it took my mind off everything."

"Oh my gosh." I reach out to hold her hand. "Why didn't you tell me?"

"Um, I think you had enough of your own shit going on." She looks at me. "Kallie, I can't even begin to think how you feel being here around him."

"It's fine." I shrug. "It is what it is, and I have to accept it."

"Accepting it and having it flaunted in your face every second is enough to have you jump off a bridge." She takes a sip of her wine.

"If only there was a bridge I could jump off," I joke with her. I don't tell her that I've cried every single night. I don't tell her that no matter how many times I tell myself not to think about him, it usually lasts maybe three minutes before another memory I've buried assaults me. I don't tell her that I moved out of my bedroom and into the spare room at night because just the thought of sleeping in the bed we used to sleep in makes my chest get tight. I don't tell her that I've had five panic attacks since my last one. I keep it to myself, just as I have everything else.

"Seriously." She takes another sip. "He holds me all night long."

"How are you sleeping?" I ask, and she looks down at her hands.

"I've never slept better," she says softly. "I mean, I'm leaving, so it's stupid to get involved." She fidgets with the label on the wine. "Maybe it's a good thing."

"He's never going to leave the farm," I say. "It's his baby."

"I would never expect him to." She looks at me as the door opens, and the man of the hour comes in.

"Hey there," he says. Tossing his baseball hat on the table, he bends down and kisses me on the cheek, then walks to her. I'm waiting to see what she does, and instead of just waiting for him to kiss her, she tilts her head, offering him her cheek. "Darlin'." His southern voice comes out.

"Casey." She says his name, and he looks at me.

"I didn't do anything." I hold up my hands.

"I want to go out," Olivia says, and Casey puts his head back and rubs his face. "I want to get out of here and go out and see people."

"You see people here," Casey says, going to the fridge and grabbing a water bottle. "You can come down to the barn."

"Casey." She gets up, and I have to say she is dressing more country. She wears her tight blue jeans and tank top. Her hair is piled on top of her head, and she has just a touch of mascara on. I want to point out the ways she has actually changed in the past four days, but I'm not sure she is ready for it. "I want to go out and I don't know, dance."

Casey looks over at me. "Listen, I don't know what to tell you."

"We can go ..." She snaps her fingers. "Line dancing."

Casey and I both groan. "There has to be a bar in this town."

"Oh, there is a bar, all right," I say, and her eyes light up. "We actually can go."

"I don't think you want to go there," Casey says, avoiding my eyes.

"Oh, come on," I say, getting up. "I know that I'll see people."

"Kallie." He says my name, but Olivia puts her hand on his mouth.

"Casey, I have cabin fever," she tells him. "I used to live in LA where I sat in traffic for four hours a day, and I am sadly missing it."

"She's right," I say, and he looks as though he is going to admit defeat.

"You are going to be there with us," Olivia says. "We can't be safer since you are going to be there. Come on, cowboy."

"Fuck me," he says and looks at me. "I don't think this is a good idea."

"I don't think it can get worse than the diner," I say. He starts to talk, and I hold up my hand. "I don't think I have anymore tears to cry. I'm dehydrated. There is nothing I can do to change the past."

"There is just something," he says, and Olivia stops him this time by grabbing his face and kissing him. "Darlin'."

"What time do I have to be ready?" Olivia asks, clapping her hands with excitement. "I don't know if I have anything to wear."

"You have seventy-five pounds of clothes all over my closet," Casey says. "I'm sure there is something there."

"I can move it to the other closet if you like." She folds her arms over her chest, and he glares at her. "I can also sleep in the room also." She turns and grabs her glass of wine, heading to the master bedroom.

"Where are you going?" he shouts.

She looks over her shoulder. "I'm going to finish my wine." She smiles. "Then I'm going to nap because I'm going to get dressed up and dance my ass off tonight." She laughs all the way to the bedroom.

"How much trouble can she possibly get into?" Casey looks at me, and I shut my laptop.

"You do see what she looks like, right?" I ask, and he doesn't say anything. "You also see what she wears." His jaw gets tight. "She is friendly with everyone. She did bring muffins to you and the boys in the barn."

"I think I need backup," he says and grabs his hat. "I don't want you to encourage her."

"If you think anything I say can encourage her"—I point at the bedroom—"then you are so oblivious." I shake my head. "I'm going home."

"You can work here," he tells me, walking out with me and closing the door behind me.

"I need a nap," I say. "Apparently, I'm going to have to dance my ass off tonight with her."

"This is a bad idea," he says, and I look at him.

"Then why did you agree to it?" I laugh and walk away from him.

"Because it made her smile," he says, and I turn around, walking backward.

"Hope you know what you're doing, big brother," I say, and he shakes his head.

"It's only temporary," he says, turning to walk back to the barn. I walk back to the house, and the smell of banana bread fills the house. My mother looks up from the oven where she's placing the muffins on the plate when I walk into the room.

"Mom, I swear by the time I go home, I'm going to have gained twenty pounds," I say, putting down my laptop and walking over to the bowl that holds the muffins from this morning.

"You can use a little bit of meat," she tells me and takes off the oven mitt. "Are you done for the day already?"

"No." I take a piece of the muffin top and toss it into my mouth. "I am going to take a nap and then work after."

"Did you not sleep well?" my mother asks with worry all over her face. "We should get another mattress for that bedroom."

"I'm sleeping okay," I say, "but Casey just agreed to take us out tonight."

She smiles at me. "That sounds like fun. You guys going to go bowling?"

I shake my head and look down, then ask the question I've been dying to ask her for the past four days. "Why didn't you tell me?"

"Tell you what?" She looks at me as I put the muffin down.

"That he didn't marry her." I wipe away a tear and look at her.

"Honey," she says, coming over to me and hugging me, "you told me that you didn't want to know. That what Jacob did with his life had nothing to do with you. Every single time I brought it up, even in passing, you changed the subject."

"It just doesn't make sense," I say. "Why wouldn't he marry her?"

"Maybe he didn't love her," my mother says, and I shake my head.

"So he just wanted to have sex with her?" I let out a breath. "I'm going to go lie down." Turning, I walk toward the stairs.

"Kallie." I stop on the second step. "One of these days, you'll have to have a conversation with him."

I swallow past the lump in my throat. "Maybe, someday."

Turning, I run up the stairs and away from the conversation she wants to have.

The nap lasts twenty minutes, and I eat almost nothing for dinner, wondering how tonight is going to play out. Maybe going out isn't such a great idea, but here I am, getting ready for tonight.

I stare at my reflection in the mirror. I left my hair loose, just curling it and then running my hands through it so it looks like a soft wave. I don't put on any eye shadow, opting for just a touch of mascara.

A soft knock sounds on the door, and I step out of my bathroom as the door opens. "Okay, this is the most country I have," Olivia says, and I shake my head.

"There is nothing country about that outfit," I say, pointing at her blue jeans and a black off-the-shoulder sweetheart shirt that shows just a touch of her toned midriff with matching platform wedges. Her blond hair is perfectly done, and her makeup is lighter than usual.

"Well, this is as country as I get," she says, shrugging. "You, on the other hand. You can take the girl out of the country, but you can't take the country out of the girl."

I laugh down at my own outfit. My blue jeans are low riding, and I've paired them with a tight flowery spaghetti strap crop top with a built-in bra, my big brown belt, and matching cowboy boots. I don't want to think about the last time I wore these boots, which was when I was going to prom.

"Well, shall we?" I say, and she nods her head with a huge smile on her face. Casey groans when he sees us coming down.

He drags his feet to the truck, opening the back door for me and the front door for Olivia. "Thank you, cowboy," she says, getting on her tippy toes and kissing his cheek.

"I don't have a good feeling about tonight," Casey says, getting into the truck and making his way over to the bar.

The parking lot is full, and I whistle when I hear the music coming from inside. "This definitely has changed from the last time I was here," I say, seeing the flash of lights coming out of the window.

"New owner came in and changed things. Put in a pool table, a dartboard, and then brought in a DJ and a band on Friday and Saturday nights," Casey says as we walk to the front door. "She also expanded, tripling the size."

"Wow," I say when he opens the door, and I step in. He was not kidding about the changes. About twenty people are already on the dance floor doing a line dance. Wooden tables are all around the dance floor, and looking past the dance floor, I see the back room is almost full of people playing pool and others watching. "This is so cool," I say, looking at Casey right before I turn fully and see her behind the bar. Smiling, she tosses a bottle up in the air and then pours it into the shot glasses in front of her. "What the ...?" I say softly, and she must sense that I'm looking at her because she looks right at me, and her smile fades. "Casey?"

"Meet the owner," he says, motioning to the bar, "Savannah."

I'm about to turn and walk out when the door opens behind us, and just like that, it's prom night all over again.

Fifteen

JACOB

"Why are you here again?" Beau asks as we walk into the bar. "Now don't get me wrong, I'm always here, but you ..." He laughs. "You never ever come here."

"Let's just say I'm working," I say, not bothering to tell him about a phone call I got this afternoon.

"What's wrong?" I answered the phone after seeing Casey's name.

"We have a situation," he said, and I sat up at my desk. We had come up empty with the mystery guy. "The girls are making me take them dancing."

"Dancing?" I repeated, making sure I had heard him right the first time.

"Kallie wants to go to the bar," he said, his voice lowering.

"But ..." I didn't know what else to say.

"I tried to tell her, but she cut me off every time." He sounded defeated. "I'm giving you a heads-up."

"I'll meet you there," I said and hung up and then called Beau.

Now here I am walking toward the place I never go to. Especially not on a Friday or Saturday night. I pull open the door, and I'm shocked to come face-to-face with the woman who has my insides all twisted up. Who is everywhere. She's on my mind when I wake up in the morning. She's on my mind no matter what I do. She's even in my dreams. I look at her, and my mouth hits the floor. I look over at Casey, and I want to ask what the fuck is he thinking taking her to go out like this.

"Well, this just got interesting," Beau says beside me as he walks in to hug Kallie. I want to yank him back by his T-shirt and hopefully choke him at the same time. "Aren't you a sight for sore eyes?"

"If you touch her again, I'll make you blind," I mumble under my breath. When Olivia chuckles, I have to wonder if I said that out loud.

"We should get a drink," Olivia says, looking at Casey. "Can you get me a drink, cowboy?" She stands in front of him, and I have to wonder what is going on with him. It's no secret he knocks boots, but he's never been seen with a woman out.

"Whatcha want, darlin'?" he asks, and she shrugs her shoulders. "Okay," he says. Then he grabs the back of her head and pulls her to him, and he kisses her on the mouth, leaving no mistake that she's his.

"I'll be back. Get a table," he says, turning and walking away while Olivia puts her hand to her lips.

"What the hell was that?" She looks at Kallie, who just throws her head back and laughs, making her breasts stick out even more. There should be a dress code in here.

"That," she says, pointing at Casey, "was him throwing down." Olivia just looks at her. "He's making sure that everyone knows you're off-limits."

"Are you saying he just marked me," she asks, ticked, "like a dog that pees on a fire hydrant?"

"More or less," Kallie tells her. "Now let's get a table, and then I can show you a two-step dance." She turns and looks at Beau. "See you later." She turns and sways away, her ass molded in her jeans. With the way her hair swings from side to side, you see that the back of her top is a corset with the bow tied at the bottom. She was a girl when she left, but there is no mistaking that Kallie Barnes is all woman now.

"I know you don't want to hear this," Beau says, "but Jesus fuck, Kallie is—"

"I'll rip your tongue out of your mouth if you finish that sentence," I say and look around to see Grady and a couple of the guys here. After I called Beau, I called a couple of the guys in and told them I needed extra eyes with me tonight, and I wasn't wrong. The place is packed with people coming from two towns away.

Savannah took her little dream and made it a reality. Besides Ethan, this is her second love. I just hope no one ever finds out how she really bought this place. I look at the bar and see Casey talking to some of the guys who work for him. They follow him to the table where the girls are sitting. Some people stop to say hi to Kallie as the music just gets louder.

"It's like she's a sitting duck," Grady says from beside me all of a sudden, and I nod. "Is it safe to assume she's off-limits?" I just look at him, and he holds up his hands with a bottle of beer in one of them. "Enough said." What the fuck is it that all the men around me want to get to know her?

Following Beau, I make my way to the bar as he sits on the stool at the end of the bar. No one sits on that stool but him. Savannah actually keeps it behind the bar, and he gets it when he comes in.

"What can I get you?" Savannah asks, and I watch Beau take a big swallow when she leans forward and you see the lace bra she's wearing under her tank top.

"I'll have a beer," I say, and Beau just nods. "That was cool," I say, "real cool."

"Shut up." Beau comes back with, and I lean on the bar and turn to look out. I scan the room, but my eyes go directly to Kallie again. She takes the shot one of the men hands her, tossing it back and then slamming the shot glass on the table. The guys high-five her while Casey looks around at his boys, and then his eyes find mine. He just nods his head, letting me know he's watching, too.

I grab the bottle of beer at the same time she grabs another shot and drink it while the song changes and the guitar comes on. Kallie jumps out of her chair and grabs Olivia's hand, leading her to the dance floor. Casey follows them along with the guys who cheer when Kallie stands in the front and looks over at Olivia. Her smile on her face is everything. Her whole face lights up, and I have to say it's the first time I've seen her actually smile in eight years. She kicks her foot forward, and Olivia mimics her, and then she rotates her hips right and left, and my cock suddenly springs to action like he has missed his long-lost best friend.

Kallie puts her right hand on her hip while the other hand goes up, and she swings her hips again. Her hair goes back and forth while she dances. She turns to the other side, both hands on her hips, while she two-steps side to side. She throws her head back and laughs when she turns to the other side and comes face-to-face with Olivia, who is trying her best to keep up. They take three steps forward, and she slaps her hip and her tits just bounce, and I can hardly stand it. One of the guys Casey knows steps up next to her. Olivia gives up and moves to stand next to Casey, who puts his arms around her shoulders. I look back and see the guys laughing with Kallie while she dances.

The whole dance floor moves in sync as she stands in the middle and takes it over. Guys who don't know her and are not from this town step up and watch. She finishes one dance and then goes into another, and when the third song comes on, she walks off the dance floor, clapping her hands. She makes her way back to their table and grabs a bottle of beer sitting on it. I shake my head. Anyone could have put something in it. Anyone could have switched it, and she would know nothing.

She drinks the bottle in one go and then hands it to Casey, and he nods his head and makes his way back to the bar. "I'll get three more and a round of shots." Savannah nods at him and then he looks at me. "What?"

"She just drank that beer that was sitting on the table this whole time, and you didn't even stop her," I say, shaking my head. "Someone could have switched it, and you wouldn't even know it until she hit the floor."

"I had eyes on it the whole time." He then leans in. "She's my sister after all."

"Yeah, except your back was to the table for three minutes," I point out, "while you watched your woman dance." The music changes, and I look over at Kallie and see a guy walk up to her and ask her to dance. Savannah hands Casey his beer and then tells him the waitress will bring the shots to him. He nods at her and turns to walk back to the table and stops when he spots Kallie walking to the dance floor. He looks over at me, and I'm standing now. Beau must sense it next to me when he gets up, and I walk to the side of the dance floor.

The guy who I've never seen before must tell her his name, and I want to close down the fucking bar. They hold hands, and he twirls her while other men hoot from the side. The dance lasts longer than I like, and when the song is over, she smiles at him and walks back to the table. I see Casey say something to her, and she just shakes her head. The guy, on the other hand, walks off the dance floor, and his friends are there to high-five him. "What the fuck? Is this high school?"

"It's called getting the hot girl to two-step," Beau says.

"They are here every Friday and Saturday." He motions to the group of guys on the side. "Usually leaving with a different girl each time."

"I don't know how you do this every single weekend." I shake my head, and then I look over at the bar and see Savannah dancing. "Okay, fine, I get it now."

"I leave with her to make sure she's safe every single time," Beau says, bringing the beer to his lips. The band gets on the stage, and the lights change, and everyone cheers when they play the first verse of "Body Like a Back Road."

Kallie puts her hands up, taking a shot from the tray. Grabbing Olivia, she leads them to the dance floor that is full now as they dance with each other. The both of them are oblivious of how much attention they are getting. "Fifty bucks someone asks her to leave with them." Beau leans over, and I side-eye him. "I'm not saying she'll go with them. I'm just saying ..."

"You can stop talking about now," I say, and for the next fucking hour, she doesn't stop dancing and neither does Olivia. And when one of the guys from the side moves up to Olivia and puts his hands on her hips, I know Casey's going to lose his shit.

"Shit," Beau says from beside me. Grady is already halfway to the scene when Casey says something to the guy. He turns around, and you can see he's drunk as he sways and then attempts to punch Casey. "Get Kallie. I'll take care of this," Grady says and I nod at him as we make our way closer.

Casey ducks and then punches the man in the jaw, making his friends jump in. Grady gets into it with a couple of them as I make eye contact with Casey who nods at me. He grabs Olivia by the hand and drags her out at the same time I get to Kallie's side and grab her around her waist, pulling her out right before the guy from before tries to grab her.

She looks over her shoulder in fear until she sees it's me as the brawl continues. I think someone throws a chair before we make it to the parking lot. "You can let me go now," Kallie says, trying to push herself away from me. "Jacob, you can let go."

"I knew this was a bad idea." I don't let her go, and if I could toss her over my shoulder and run to my truck, I would. I see Casey's truck take off, and he looks at me and nods. "Told him it was a bad idea."

"What the hell, Jacob?" she says, and with my hand on her skin, I don't see anything else.

"You could have gotten hurt in there," I say when I stop beside my truck and open the door, finally letting her go, "but did you stop and think of that?"

"It's none of your business," she hisses.

"Get in the truck, Kallie." I don't give her enough room to do anything but get in the truck.

"No fucking way," she says and looks around.

"Fine by me," I say. Picking her up, I put her in the truck so fast she is in shock. "I dare you to run," I say, getting so close I can feel her breath on my face. "I didn't catch you eight years ago," I say, my eyes going to her parted lips as her chest rises and falls, "but I'm not going to make that mistake again."

Sixteen

KALLIE

It all happened so fast it's a whirlwind, even thinking about it now. For the first time, I didn't care that I was back in my old town. I didn't care that people were probably sitting there just to see how I would react. I didn't care that tomorrow my mother's phone would be ringing off the hook with stories about tonight.

I got on that dance floor and left all my problems at the door. I kicked up my cowboy boots and loved every single minute of it. Knowing deep inside I was pushing things, but I didn't think anything of it. Nothing happens in this town, but oh, how I was wrong.

The whole night, Casey was right there beside us, making sure we were okay, his jaw clenching each time Olivia would swing her hips. His eyes were glaring when someone would get too close. I snickered to myself more than once and then all hell broke loose.

I was almost pushed to the side, but then suddenly I felt hands around my waist, and for the first time tonight, fear set in. That is, until I looked over my shoulder and saw Jacob.

My heart sped up, and it wasn't because I heard a brawl right behind me. No, it was speeding up because Jacob was touching me, and there was nothing I could do about it. My head hated him, yet my heart loved him. The warm air hit me right away when we got outside, and I thought for sure he would let me go. I was banking on it, but he didn't. All he did was mumble to himself.

"What the hell, Jacob?" Words finally come out, and I curse at him.

"You could have gotten hurt in there." Stopping, he puts me down right next to his truck and opens the door. In the darkness of the night, the lights from the stars and full moon shine on his face, and I see the anger. Anger and a mix of something else. Something I'm not sure I want to know. "But did you stop and think of that?"

"It's none of your business," I hiss; the nerve of him.

Apparently, in the eight years I've been away, Jacob's patience was cut thin. "Get in the truck, Kallie." He advances on me, not giving me enough room to do anything but get in the truck. I try to waste time, thinking Casey is going to come out any minute now with Olivia over his shoulder, and he'll save me.

"No fucking way." Shaking my head, I look around.

"Fine by me," he says, and then I know he isn't joking. His tone made it clear he was done having a discussion with me. One second, I'm standing here, and the next, his hands are around my waist and picking me up like I'm light as a feather and putting me in the passenger seat. All I can do is look at him in shock that he just did that. He gets so close to me that I have to hold my breath. "I dare you to run." His tone is fierce and menacing. "I didn't catch you eight years ago," he finally says, and my mouth opens at that. "But I'm not going to make that mistake again."

He slams the door closed, and I'm stuck here in the seat as if he put crazy glue down, and I can't move. He gets into the truck and starts it and pulls out of the parking lot. We see Casey pulling out at the same time, and all they do is nod at each other. He turns down the pitch-black road, and he presses his Bluetooth to call Casey. He answers after one ring, and his voice is tight. "What?"

"Just giving you a heads-up that Kallie isn't going home right away," he says, and my head snaps up to him.

"What the fuck are you talking about, Jacob?" Casey says, and all Jacob does is disconnect the call.

"Jacob, I want you to take me home," I say, and he just shakes his head.

"There are things that need to be said," he says, and then he makes his way to the creek. I know he's going there.

"We can talk tomorrow over coffee." My hand holds onto the door for dear life. My heart is beating so fast all I can do is hear the echoes in my ears.

He doesn't say anything to me when he parks the car and turns off the light, and he turns to look at me with his back to the door. "Kallie, we can do this one of two ways. The easy way or the hard way."

"I don't even know what that means," I say, opening the door and jumping out of his truck. "Honest to God, Jacob, I have no idea what that means."

The sound of his door closing fills the silent air. "Aren't you tired of running?" he asks.

"Fuck you, Jacob," I spew at him and turn to walk toward the creek. "Let's get this over with so I can go home and forget tonight."

During the whole walk to the creek, I just get angrier at the nerve of him demanding this shit and the audacity of him forcing me to do this. "I don't know why we have to do this," I finally say when I hear the creek. "There really isn't much to say."

"What are you talking about?" he says.

I see the rock, and I stop and turn around to look at him. I don't why looking at him gets my stomach fluttering. I don't know why there is suddenly a lump in my throat. Maybe it's because he's going to say things I don't want to hear. "I'm talking about this conversation. It's pretty much self-explanatory."

"Is it?" He puts his hands in his back pockets, and his chest is so much bigger for some reason. Or maybe it's the darkness or the shadows.

"It is." Folding my arms over my chest, I say, "Everything that we had was a lie."

"What?" he asks, shocked.

"So how long were you fucking Savannah?" I ask, ignoring the lump in my throat and the tears burning my eyes. "Was it the whole time?"

"It's not what you think," he says, and I shake my head.

"Eight years!" I shout. "After eight fucking years, all you can come up with is it's not what you think?"

"Kallie." He hisses my name, and I get even more angry. My stomach feels like a tsunami is in it with all the nerves I have.

"I'm here, Jacob." I throw my hands up. "This is what you wanted to talk about it. Well, I'm asking my questions."

"It's not that easy," he says softly and looks down.

"When did it happen?" I ask what I've been asking myself for the last eight years. "When? Was it in my face the whole time?" He shakes his head. "That's it? That's all you got?"

"All I can say is it's not what you think," he says, and I now lose the battle of my tears.

"When did you fall out of love with me?" I ask him softly.

"Never," he says, his voice almost a whisper, and I have to laugh.

"Why?" I ask. "Why did you do it? Why didn't you just break up with me?" My voice cracks, and he takes a step closer to me, but I take a step back. "Why, Jacob?" I put my hand in front of my trembling lips. "Why didn't you marry her?"

"Because she wasn't you," he says. Standing right in front of me, he places his hands on my face as he holds me there with his eyes on mine. "I've never loved anyone but you," he says, and the tears roll over my rims and onto his thumbs. He brings his head closer to mine. "I've loved you my whole life," he says right before his lips hit mine, and my hands go to his waist.

I've dreamed of this kiss every single day, no matter how much I told myself that I hated him. He would creep into my dreams, dreams that were filled with kisses. But nothing can compare to his real kiss.

His tongue mixes with mine, and my body gives in to him. I kiss him with everything that I have. I take and give him everything that I've wanted to in the past eight years. My head moves from right to left, and his hands go from my face to my hair as he steps closer to me. Our chests press together, his tongue fighting with mine over and over again.

I get lost in him, just as I always have. I get lost in the feel of him. I get lost in the love I have for him. "Kallie." He whispers my name, and that memory of eight years ago flashes again in my mind.

"Jacob." I blink once, twice, three times. I step out of his touch, and I look at him. "It's over."

"What?" he whispers.

"This." I point at my chest and then at his. "This is over."

"Never." He shakes his head.

"It was over the minute you touched her," I say, and then I

look down at the ground and then up again. "It was over the minute you lied to me."

"I never lied to you," he says, his voice broken. "Never."

"It is what it is, Jacob." My voice comes out monotone, matching my heart. "Please don't follow me." I turn to walk away and stop turning. For eight years, I've hated him in my head, and for eight years, I dreamed of this moment to confront him. I thought I was going to be stronger, thought I would be a hard ass and demand answers. "For eight years, I've thought of this, right here. I thought that you could give me answers. I thought you could tell me, but now I know it doesn't matter. Nothing matters because in the end you chose her." I shrug now, keeping the sob at bay. "It would have been magical," I say. "It would have been everything that I've ever dreamed of."

"What would?" he asks, and I see a tear roll down his cheek.

"Our life." I take one last look at him, and then I turn to make my way back to my house. I shed all of my tears, or what I feel are all my tears. Walking past the barn, I see that the only light on at Casey's house is the porch light. I turn to walk toward my parents' house, and I walk up the five steps to the porch, but instead of going into the house, I kick off my boots and walk to the porch swing. Sitting on the swing, I look off into the darkness of the night. My head hangs forward, suddenly too heavy to hold up.

The door creaks open, and I look over to see my mother coming out. She's dressed in a white plush robe I sent her last year for Christmas. "Did I wake you?"

"No," she says to me, coming over and sitting next to me, holding my hand in hers. My head falls to her shoulder. "Jacob called."

"I love him," I say softly.

"I know, baby," she says, and I look at her and see she has

her own tears running down her face. Leaning back, she lets go of my hand to put her arm around my shoulder, and I lie down with my head in her lap. She plays with my hair as she swings us.

"Tomorrow," I say softly, my eyes getting heavy. "Tomorrow I'll work on not loving him."

Seventeen

JACOB

She stood there in front of me, each word stabbing me in the chest. Each time, I wanted to tell her the biggest secret of my life. Each time, I wanted to take her in my arms. Yet each time, the lie stopped me.

The kiss was everything that I remember but even better. I haven't kissed anyone in eight years. I haven't touched anyone in eight years. I haven't because no one could measure up to her.

"It is what it is, Jacob." Her voice came out like there was nothing left inside her. The fight was gone. "Please don't follow me." She turns and walks away from me, and I'm about to take a step toward her when she stops and turns around and looks at me. "For eight years, I've thought of this, right here. I thought that you could give me answers. I thought you could tell me, but now I know it doesn't matter. Nothing matters because in the end you chose her." She shrugs, and I want to fucking shout that it's not true. That I would never do anything to hurt her. "It would have been magical," she tells me. "It would have been everything that I've ever dreamed up."

"What would?" I ask, and now my own tears start to come.

"Our life," she whispers and walks away from me. My legs actually give out on me, and I fall to my knees. I take out my phone and call the number I will always remember.

"Hello," Charlotte says, answering the phone after one ring.

"Hey, it's Jacob," I say, my voice breaking.

"What happened?" she asks me, frantically, and I hear the covers rustle.

"I ..." I start, "Kallie is on her way home."

"Okay," she says in a whisper.

"I'm going to make sure she gets there okay, but I won't be with her."

"I'll be watching," she says. Just as I'm about to hang up the phone, I hear, "Thank you, Jacob."

Putting the phone in my pocket, I climb to my feet slowly and follow her back to her house. Never once getting close enough for her to know I'm there. The twigs cracking under her shoes is the only sound I hear.

She walks to the house, and when I see her kick off her boots and sit on the swing with her head hanging, anger and rage fill me because I did that to her. The woman with the most beautiful smile in the world sits with her head hanging because I just broke her again.

Turning, I make my way back to my truck and start it. I'm headed home when I turn back at the last minute. I pull up to the house, and the lights are all off. I knock on the door once, twice, and then the third time when I see the light in the hallway turn on.

I turn my back to the door and look out into the darkness of the night. When I hear the door unlock, I turn and look at Savannah, who looks like she was dead asleep. "Jacob?" She says my name with confusion. "What's wrong?" She pulls her robe closer together.

"I was with Kallie tonight," I say, "and she asked me when I fell out of love with her."

"Jacob," Savannah says softly, and she comes out of the doorway.

I take a step back. "She asked all the questions that I would ask her if the roles were reversed. She said I chose you over her."

"I'm so sorry," she says and shakes her head.

"She asked me all these fucking questions, and all I could answer her was it's not what you think," I say. "That's all I could give her."

"What do you want me to say?" Savannah asks, and it's my turn now to ask her.

"I'm asking you permission to tell her." I look down. "I promised you that I would keep your secret." My heart speeds up.

"Jacob, what if she told someone?" she asks. "Everything will be ruined. Ethan will be thrown in this mess."

"You think I don't know that!" I shout at her now, angry with her. "You think this hasn't crossed my mind in eight years? He is my son, mine." I point at my chest. "Nothing will take that away from me and away from him." I swallow. "I'm asking you to give me this, Savannah," I plead with her. "Give me my life back. I beg you to give me back what you took from me."

"I never wanted you to be caught up in this. I never wanted you to lose her. I know that losing her broke you, and I know that you blame me, even if you say you don't. It's why you flinch when I touch you. It's why you won't look me in the eye."

"She's my everything," I say. "I thought I hated her for

leaving, but I can't." I rub my chest. "I love her with every-thing I have, and I want her. I want my life back."

"What about Ethan?" she asks me with tears now running down her face. "Where is he in all this?"

"Ethan is my son, and nothing will take that away," I say. "Nothing."

"Then tell her," she says softly. Turning, she walks back in the house, closes the door, and locks it. The light in the house turns off, and I sit on the steps of the house. I don't know how long I sit here, but when I get up, the sun is rising. I get in my truck and make my way back to Kallie.

I pull up to the front of her house, and Charlotte opens the front door right away and says, "Thought you would have been here earlier." She's still in her robe. I know she hasn't been back to sleep since I called her.

"Where is she?" I ask, and she looks at me.

"She's asleep on the back swing," she tells me. "What are you going to do?"

"Something I should have done eight years ago," I say honestly. "Fight for her."

"It's not going to be easy," she says, wiping away a tear from her cheek. "She just came back. I can't lose her again."

"I know nothing I can say will make you believe me."

"Actions speak louder than words." I nod at her and walk around the house to the back porch. Kallie lies there with her hair sprawled all around her, and you can see her cheeks stained with tears. I walk up the steps as quietly as I can and crouch down in front of the swing.

I look at her sleeping, and all I can do is watch. My hand comes out without me thinking, and my thumb rubs her cheek. She stirs under me for a second, but her eyes stay closed. I play with her hair, and she finally opens her eyes. "Jacob." She whispers my name, confused. "What are you doing here?"

"I need you to come with me," I say, and she just looks at me with big tears in her eyes. "It's the last thing I will ever ask you."

"We said everything that needs to be said," she says and sits up. "It's just too much."

"I didn't say what I need to say," I say. "I'm asking you to give me the chance to tell you everything."

"You had your chance," she says as she stands. "Just leave me."

"I can't," I say, standing in front of her. "Just give me this chance."

"If I give you this one chance," she says, "promise me that after this, you will leave me alone."

There is no way in fuck I can promise that or would, but I know that if I don't, she won't come with me, so I lie to her for the first time ever. "I promise."

"I need to change. I'll meet you in the front," she says. I nod my head and watch as she picks up her boots and goes inside the house.

I'm about to walk to the front of the house when I see Casey walking toward me with a white coffee cup in his hand. His eyes narrow on me. "What are you doing here?" he asks me when he gets close enough. "She walked home by herself."

"She was never by herself," I say and look at the ground. "I was following her. I was just giving her space."

"Not enough space if you're here again," he says, taking a sip of his coffee.

"Well, if I get my way, you'll be seeing my face daily," I say, and I don't wait for him to answer. Instead, I walk to the front and wait for her beside my truck. When the door opens and she steps out, my breath hitches like every other time. She's wearing white shorts this time with a beige top showing off her stomach, and she's carrying a thermos cup in each hand.

Her hair blows softly in the wind. I open the door for her, and she hands me a coffee.

"My mother sent this for you," she says and climbs in the truck. I wait for her to sit before I close the door, then I walk to my side of the truck. Looking up at the front door where Charlotte stands, I just nod at her. I get in the car and hear her take a deep inhale. "Let's get this over with."

"Let's," I say, and I make my way to my house. She has never been to my house, and I'm hoping that she doesn't refuse to come in, but with the secret I have to tell her, there is no way I could do it out in the open. As much as I love her, I still have to protect my son, and having the secret out into the world will put him in more danger than I care to think about.

I pull up to my house and press the button for the garage and drive in. "I thought we were going to do this at the creek," she says softly beside me.

"What I need to tell you can't be said there," I say, and she looks down at the cup in her hand.

"Is this your house?" she asks me and then looks at me.

"Yes," I say. "Give me fifteen minutes, and if you still want to leave, I'll take you home."

She debates a bit and then opens the door. I get out with her and wait for her at the stairs that lead to the mud room. I open the door for her and wait for her to step in, and she doesn't move from the entryway.

"This way," I say and lead her from the mud room through the white kitchen toward the family room. It's the room where we spend all our time. Her eyes roam around the room toward the back wall that holds the fireplace and the television on top of it, but her eyes pause on the framed pictures on the built-in shelves. Ethan's first day at school. His first Christmas. Pictures of us fishing together. The pictures are all there, but one thing is clear. This is where I live with my son.

"I'm here," she says, trying not to make eye contact with me. "What do you have to say?" I take a deep breath, and for the first time, I tell her my side of the story.

Eighteen

KALLIE

I fell asleep with his kiss on my lips and my heart heavier than it's ever been before. What I wasn't expecting was for him to be there with me when I got up.

His eyes shine as he watched me, asking him to give him a chance to tell his side of the story. *It was too little, too late*, my brain screamed while my heart said to give him this one chance. I got in his truck with my mother's words lingering in my mind. "He isn't the only one keeping secrets, Kallie."

No, he wasn't, and before this day was over, he would know my secret. He would know it all. I looked out the window, watching the trees pass us by without saying a word, not realizing we were going so far out of the way until we pulled up to a white house with wooden slates around the big windows. We pull into the garage, and I know we are at his house. His house where he lives with his child and God knows who else. I don't want to get out, but we need to have this talk. I follow him to the mud room, and I try not to look around and invade his privacy. We walk past the white kitchen on one side and a dining room table on the other with eight chairs. A schoolbag sits in the middle of the table with some papers stacked on top.

We walk into the family room, and my eyes go to the pictures on the shelves. Pictures of his life with his son. I try to calm my heart as I feel a panic attack coming on. *In and out*, I tell myself.

"I'm here," I say to him, not looking at him. "What do you have to say?" He takes a deep breath, and I look at him.

"Jesus," he says, putting his hand on his neck and looking up at the ceiling. "I've gone over this speech so many times in my head, but now that it's here, I don't even know where to start," he says and laughs, but a tear comes out of his eyes. "Before I even start, I want to make one thing clear. I've never ever stopped loving you, even when I didn't want to."

"I think I need to sit down," I say and slowly sit on the couch, facing him. He sits on the couch and rests his elbows on his knees. "You asked me before the biggest question, when did it happen?" he starts, and I suddenly think I'm going to be sick. Maybe I don't want to know this. Maybe I should just accept that they were together. "The answer to that is—"

"Stop," I say, and I silently sob. "I know I wanted to know, but I don't think I can."

"Never," he whispers, and my head snaps back. "Never." He shakes his head as tears pour out of him. "I was never with her."

"What?" I ask him as my head spins. "I don't …"

"Savannah came to me the night of prom and told me she was pregnant," he says, his legs shaking now. "I was shocked. I had no idea she was dating anyone, let alone with someone." I don't know if I'm actually hearing this properly. "She was scared, petrified actually, and she had no idea what to do. Her mother was …" I put my hand up because I know exactly what her mother was. "She asked me to help her, and it just happened so fast. My head was spinning, and then you were there in front of me, and the whispers were already starting."

"You stood there in front of me and admitted it," I say, angry with him, and I jump up.

"I never admitted anything, Kallie," he says softly. "Trust me, you think I forgot the moment my world shattered around me? I never said it was mine. I never ever said those words."

"But you said you could explain," I say, the night coming back to me. "Why would you need to explain anything if it wasn't yours?" I sit back down, looking into the same eyes of the man who stood in front of me eight years ago begging to let him explain.

"You made me believe you cheated on me," I say now, getting back up again and going to the fireplace where I can walk back and forth and make sense of what he just said to me. "You made me doubt everything!" I yell. "You fucking broke me. Why?"

"She was desperate," he says. "Her back was against the wall, and she was drowning. After you left town, I figured I had nothing else left. There was no reason to tell my side of the story, so I kept her secret."

"Who knows?" I ask.

"My father," he says, and my hand goes to my mouth, "and you."

"What about Beau?" I ask. "Surely, the three musketeers would fill him in on that secret."

"There is no way that we could tell him," he says and looks down and then up. "It's Liam's."

"You have got to be fucking kidding me!" I shout, and I want to throw something, break something. "This whole fucking thing is a—"

"Yeah," he says, cutting me off.

"You chose her," I say softly. "Out of all this, you chose her."

"I never chose her," he tells me, getting up. "I chose Ethan." He says his name, and I look at him with tears in his eyes. "In all this, I chose my son."

When he says the words, my body starts to shake. I start to shake. "Your son," I whisper.

"Yeah, I have a son," he says. I look at him, and at that moment, everything comes out of me.

"You have two sons," I whisper, my secret now free from Pandora's box.

"What?" he says, getting up now and looking at me. "What did you say?"

He gave me his truth, and now it's time to give him mine. "I said you have two sons."

"Oh my God," he says, putting his hands to his mouth.

"I found out I was pregnant a month after I left. I was beside myself. I lost so much weight. I was sleeping and vomiting. I couldn't keep anything down. I just thought I was depressed." I don't stop, knowing that if I stop, I won't have the courage to continue. "My mother came and finally forced me to go to the doctor. I was twelve weeks along. They turned off the lights in the small white room and put gel on my stomach, and then I saw our son for the first time. His heartbeat was strong, and at that moment, I knew that whatever you did, we created this amazing boy."

"My son." His voice is a whisper.

"It wasn't an easy pregnancy," I say. "I ate for him, I drank for him, I lived for him. My baby. My son."

"Our son," he reminds me, and I look down.

"When I was twenty-one weeks, I got a sharp cramp, and I thought it was just stomach pains." I put my hand to my stomach, feeling the emptiness. "Then the bleeding started."

"Kallie ..." He says my name, but I'm in a trance as I'm back to that day.

"I rushed to the hospital," I sob out, "calling my mother along the way, and she rushed there. When I got to the hospital, they put me in the bed, and I lay there while all this blood poured out of me. I tried to stop it, tried to close my legs, thinking it would stop it. In almost the same room that I listened to our son's heartbeat, I was told there was no more heartbeat." He roars out a sob and falls to his knees in front of me, and I want to do the same. "These things happen, they told me. I was in a state of shock by the time my mother got there. Catatonic almost, but it wasn't over. I had to deliver our child. He was perfect." I sob. "He was the most beautiful baby in the world. I held him for as long as they would let me. I told him that you loved him more than anything in the world. I told him that he had to be our angel now." The crushing blow was even more now than it was on that day. "I blamed myself for everything. If I wasn't depressed, then maybe he would have survived. If I ate more, maybe he would be okay. If I didn't cry every day, maybe he would have known how happy I was to be his mommy." I walk over to Jacob now who sobs with his hands covering his face. "So you don't have just one son, you have two."

"Kallie," he says, and I walk closer to him. He grabs my hips and puts his face to my stomach and kisses it. "I'm so sorry."

My hand goes into his hair, like I always do, my own tears falling and mixing with his. "I named him Gabriel." The sob rips through him now, and I hold Jacob in my arms as he cries for our child.

"I'm so sorry." He keeps saying that over and over again, and I look at him.

"I'm sorry for doubting you, and I'm sorry that I ran from

you." I lean in and put my forehead against his. "I was just so devastated that the only thing I could do was run."

He's about to say something else when the front door opens, and all we hear is screaming. "Dad, I'm home!" His eyes fly to mine, and then it happens in slow motion.

"Dad?" We hear again, and Ethan comes into the room with a huge smile on his face that falls when he sees me with his father. Or it falls because he sees his father in tears.

"Ethan." Jacob stands, and I want to say that it doesn't hurt me, but I'm gutted. Hearing his son call him dad and knowing that our son would be his age. I'm about to get up and excuse myself to leave when I hear Cristine.

"You have got to be kidding me," she hisses, and it's Jacob who talks now.

"Buddy, bring your bag in your room and bring me down your laundry," he tells Ethan. The little boy looks at me, and I just smile.

"Okay, Dad," he says softly and walks away. Only when Jacob knows he's out of the room does he look at his mother.

"This ends now," he tells her. "This shit. All of it."

"She deserted you in your hour of need," Cristine says. I want to tell her she's right, but instead, I excuse myself.

"I'm going to let myself out," I say, not making eye contact. I turn to walk out of the house, hoping like fuck it's an easy way to go. Luckily for me, the foyer is right in front of me, and the front door is now shining at me.

My hand grabs the door handle, and I'm about to open it when I feel his hand on mine. "You can't leave," he says, my back against his chest. "You can't just leave."

"I'm not leaving," I say, but really, I am. "I'm just ... we just have a lot to process, so I was going to go." He turns me in his arms.

"You were escaping again, and I'm not going to let you," he says.

"I just need some time," I say. "I wasn't running forever. I was just ..." I look down. "It's a lot to take in, and I just laid a lot out there for you, too. So it's a good time to go to our separate corners and talk later."

I hear the crunch of rock, and I look over to see that it's Casey. "Besides, you have Ethan here, and I just ..."

"Can I call you later?" he asks, wrapping his arms around me, and I nod at him. "Okay, then." He kisses my lips softly. "But we have to finish this conversation."

"We will," I say, and I turn to walk out of the door toward Casey, who looks at me when I get in the truck.

"What's the story?" he asks, and I look at him. "Do I need to take him out?"

I shake my head with a laugh, my heart feeling just a touch lighter. "Not today."

Nineteen

I watch her walk to Casey's truck and get in and fucking hate it. I want her to stay here with us always.

"You cannot be serious right now, Jacob," my mother says from behind me, and I take a deep breath. "You brought that woman into your home."

"That woman is going to be my wife," I say, turning around, and she takes a step back. "She just doesn't know it yet. But I'm going to make her my wife, and if you push her away, that means you'll be pushing me away."

"But ..." she starts to say. "But you have Ethan and Savannah." *And Gabriel*, I think to myself. I rub my chest where my tattoo hides. A tattoo I got when my father passed away of a cross for him and under it, I put Ethan's birthday. I am going to have to add another birthday to that. I ignore the pain in my chest as I think of my child and the pain that she went through. Alone. Without me. Doubting that what we had was real.

"I have Ethan, and Kallie knows this. It isn't a surprise to anyone," I say and walk back into the living room. "And as for Savannah, the only relationship I want with her is to co-parent with her, exactly as I have been." I walk back into the kitchen and open the fridge to start breakfast.

"But …" I lose it and slap my hand on the counter. I look to see if Ethan is in the room.

"Mom, enough," I hiss. "But nothing. Kallie is the one. She's always been the one. She will always be the one."

"I can't forgive her for leaving you," she says and looks down. "I won't."

"Then that's too bad," I say, "because I'm hoping like fuck Charlotte can forgive me for fathering a child that wasn't her daughter's." She gasps. "Now, are you staying for breakfast or not?"

"I think I am going to leave you and Ethan," my mother says. "I think you have a lot to talk about. But," she says softly, "just remember that he has a mother and doesn't need a stand-in." She turns on her heels and walks out, and I make a mental note that we are definitely going to have more words.

"Where is Grandma?" Ethan comes into the room with his basket of dirty clothes.

"She had to take off," I say and start to make breakfast while he carries his clothes to the laundry room.

"Can I watch television?" He looks at me, and I nod while I make him pancakes, bacon, and eggs. He turns off the television and comes to the island when I call him to come eat. He gets on the stool and looks over at me. "Did you and Grandma have a fight?"

"Why do you say that?" Wondering if he heard what we were arguing about, I look over at him.

"I heard her yell, and then she left." He chews a piece of pancake. "Who was that girl?"

"Grandma and I were just talking," I say, "and that girl was Kallie."

He looks at me. "Kallie and I were best friends when we were in high school."

134

"Like you and Mom and Uncle Beau?" he asks.

"She was actually my girlfriend," I say, and he looks at me and then takes another bite of his food. No doubt he's processing everything. He's always been like that.

"Where has she been?" I look over at him.

"She left for school, and she just came back," I say. "You know Casey, right?"

"Is that the cowboy?" he asks with his eyes big. "He's so cool. Last year at the county fair, he lasted the longest on the bull." I roll my eyes.

"He isn't that cool," I say, and he laughs. "But yes, that is her brother."

"Cool," he says again, picking up his eggs and then looking at me. "Are you going to start dating her again?"

I think about how to answer this. I don't want to lie to my son, but I also want to be honest with him because if I get my way, she is going to be here a lot more. "I hope so."

"Buy her candy," he says with a smile. "Lollipops for sure."

"Is that so?" I smirk at him, and he nods his head.

"I brought Alexis one, and she held my hand the whole recess," he says. "But it made my hand all sweaty and gross, so I am not going to do that again." I throw my head back and laugh. I lean over and kiss his head, and I think of our son and only then do I realize they would be the same age. Tears spring to my eyes, and I blink them away but not before he sees them. "You don't have to hold her hand if you don't want to."

"I want to hold her hand," I say, "and I want her to come over for dinners, and I want you to meet her."

"She's pretty," he says, finishing his last piece of pancake. "We should invite her for movie night."

"That is a great idea," I say and get up, grabbing our plates and rinsing them off. "Now go get your homework so we can get that over with."

He grumbles and groans while he walks to the back room

when the doorbell rings. Turning the water off, I walk to the door and see it's Savannah. I unlock the door, and she smiles at me when I step to the side to let her come in. "Hey," she says softly, "is Ethan here?"

"He is," I say, shutting the door behind her and looking at her. She looks like she hasn't slept, and you can see that she has been crying. "Is everything okay?"

"You tell me, Jacob." She stands there. "Is everything going to be okay?"

"If you're asking me if Kallie is going to tell anyone, the answer is no," I say. I didn't actually tell her not to, but I'm assuming she knows that the secret is just ours. "She wouldn't do that."

"Wouldn't she?" Savannah says. "She doesn't know what it's like being pregnant and alone."

I'm about to snap when Ethan comes in the room, and Savannah sees the glare on my face. "Mom," he says, hugging her waist, "what are you doing here?"

"I thought it would be a good weekend to go up and visit Grammy," she says of her mother who lives three towns over. She worked for Beau's parents for twenty years, and then right before Ethan was born, she hightailed it out of town, leaving her daughter pregnant and alone. The only one it surprised was Savannah.

"Can we go to the fair?" he asks, his eyes going big.

"Yeah, if they're in town, we can." She smiles at him. "Now go get your stuff."

"I'm going to win you another bear, Mom," he says with a smile and then runs to get his stuff.

"You're taking a Saturday off?" I look at her, and she shrugs.

"After the brawl last night ..." She shakes her head. "It'll take a couple of days for them to clean up and fix the holes."

"Was it that bad?" I ask, and she nods.

"It was fine until someone threw a chair, and then it went downhill," she says and then looks down. Ethan comes in the room wearing his backpack and a hat on his head. "Say bye to Dad."

"Bye, Dad," he says, and I grab his face in my hands.

"Love you, kid." I kiss his nose and then his forehead. "Call me when you get there."

"Will do," Savannah says, and I walk out of the house and watch them drive away.

I pick up my phone and call the number again, feeling nervous suddenly. It's like I'm back in high school. Charlotte answers the phone after three rings, sounding out of breath. "Hey, Mrs. Barnes."

"Hey," she says softly, and I have to wonder if Kallie told her that I now know about the baby. "How are you doing?" Her voice goes lower, and my question is answered.

"I'm doing good. Is Kallie there?" I ask, and she calls Kallie who picks up the phone.

"Hey," I say to her, and her voice is sleepy. "Were you sleeping?"

"No," she says, and I hear the blankets rustle. "Just resting."

"I was wondering if you'd like to spend the day with me?" I ask. My heart beats rapidly in my chest as I wait for her answer.

"Don't you have Ethan?"

"He just left with Savannah for the weekend," I say. "I'm sitting out on my porch, and all I can think about is you." Looking up at the sun shining in the sky, I say, "We need to finish our talk."

"Yeah," she says softly. "We were interrupted."

"If you want, I can pick you up," I say, and I'm so anxious I just want to tell her I'll be there in ten minutes.

"No, don't come all this way. I'll just take my mother's car," she tells me. "I just don't know your address."

I give her the address, and she tells me she'll be over soon. I want to ask her what soon means. Does it mean an hour, or does it mean ten minutes? Getting up, I walk to my bedroom, taking off my clothes and stepping into the shower. The hot water runs over my stiff neck muscles. My eyes burn from being up all night, so I turn the water to cold and stick my face under it.

Getting out, I grab one of the white towels and dry myself off, slipping on my boxers and shorts. I'm towel-drying my hair when I hear the doorbell. I drop the towel on the bed and walk to the front door. I see Kallie right away through the glass in the doors. Her hair is loose and falls over her shoulders. She looks down and then looks to the side, and her beauty takes my breath away. She looks in the house and sees me, and a small smile fills her face.

"Hey," I say, opening the door. "Sorry, I was just getting out of the shower." I see that she is wearing another pair of shorts, this time jeans, and the blue loose short-sleeved shirt she has on is tucked into them. Her hair hides one side of the shirt that goes off her shoulder.

Her eyes almost pop out of her head when she sees me, and I want to laugh since she's seen me naked many, many times. Maybe not in a while but I'm still the same guy. "Um," she says, trying not to blush, and her eyes go to the tattoo on my left pec. This is brand new. I got it when my father died. It's a cross with a ribbon around it with the date he died and the date Ethan was born. Under the cross is the scripture "For those I love I sacrifice."

"I'm sorry. I should have."

I grab her face in my hands and lean down to kiss her lips. "I'm happy you're here." Turning, I pull her into the house with me. "Do you want something to drink? Some sweet tea, some coffee, some water, whiskey?"

She smiles at me and shakes her head, and I notice she has a brown manila envelope with her. "I'm good," she says, and then we stop in the hallway in front of the couches.

"Are you as nervous as I am?" I ask as my heart speeds so fast I might have to sit down.

"A little more, I think." She tilts her head to the side. My hand moves to hold her neck, and I feel her heartbeat with my thumb. "Do you want to sit?" She nods her head and walks away from me, and my hand falls to my side. She sits down on one of the loveseats, and I don't know if I should sit next to her or not. Fuck, this being on pins and needles stuff is killing me.

Walking to her, I sit next to her, and she holds the envelope in her lap. I'm suddenly feeling like the room is spinning. "What do you have there?"

She looks down in her lap, and her hand caresses the envelope with a soft touch. She brings it to her chest, and the tears come out now. "Shit," she says, trying to laugh through her tears. "Maybe I should have taken the whiskey."

"Whatever it is," I say, "it'll be okay."

She nods at me. "Jacob, I'd like to show you," she says, blinking as the tears come out now, and my hand goes over to hold her knee. The tears falling on my hand, she opens the envelope and takes out a little square paper. "This is Gabriel."

Twenty

KALLIE

My hands shake like a leaf on a windy day when I take the little black and white picture out. "This is Gabriel," I say with all the pride in the world. When I went home, the first thing I did was get the envelope out. An envelope that my mother took the day she left me after we buried him. She took all but one picture that I still have in my wallet, and that no one has ever seen but me.

When I hand him the picture, he turns over the sonogram picture, and he puts his hand to his mouth to stop the sob from ripping out. "That was the first time I got to hear his heartbeat," I say, sitting closer to him so I can see the picture. Jacob just looks down at it and takes his finger and traces the baby.

"He's so beautiful," he says, and I just nod.

I open the envelope and grab the other picture, which shows him getting a bit bigger. "He was sucking his thumb here," I say, my heart feeling so full to share this with him while at the same time feeling the emptiness that always lingers there. The feeling that I'm missing a piece of me.

"Did you used to talk to him?" he asks, and I smile.

"I did. He was a great listener." I smile, thinking of the times he used to kick me just for fun. "He also loved Coke." I remember all of a sudden. "He used to go nuts in my stomach when I had it."

"I'm so sorry, Kallie," he says, looking down at the picture, and it's time to show him the last picture.

"This is the day he was born," I say and pull out the picture of him wrapped in the white sheet. "He was small but perfect." He looks like he is sleeping. You would never think otherwise.

He takes the picture out of my hand, and his shoulders start to shake as he holds the picture in his hand. His tears are dripping down his chin. "He's so beautiful." He looks at me, and I smile at him. "He looks like you."

"No," I say, shaking my head. "He looked exactly like you," I say and then hand him another picture.

He looks at it and gasps. "This is why you had the panic attack?" He doesn't ask me so much as tells me. The picture is of me holding Gabriel in my arms, my face pale as tears are running down my cheeks with my mother beside me on the hospital bed with her arm around the two of us. Her own tears are on her face. "I want to tell my mother," he says, looking at the picture. "I want to tell everyone about my son."

"I don't know," I say honestly and put the envelope down. "I haven't even told my father and Casey."

"Then we'll do it together." He grabs my hand in his. "You don't have to do anything alone anymore."

"I just don't think it's a good idea," I say. "Your mother already isn't keen on us talking."

"You gave birth to our child by yourself," he says angrily. "You buried him all by yourself. Our child," he repeats. "Our son."

"Okay," I say, "I just want to tell my father before anyone, please."

He nods his head and then looks at me. "Can I keep this?" he asks me.

"Those are for you and this also." I take out the last paper in the envelope. "It's small, but it's his footprint."

"I've never in my life felt so much yet so empty at the same time," he says to me, wiping his cheek with the back of his hand.

"I know the feeling," I say. "It's a bit better now that I get to share him with you. That you know him also."

He puts the pictures down on the table in front of him and then turns to me and pulls me to him. I straddle him, just as I did so many years ago. Just as I've remembered all these years. Except he's bigger, and his chest is wider. When he opened the door without a shirt, I thought for sure my chin would hit the floor. He was just perfect; he was always perfect in my eyes, though. He was always the best looking, always the funniest, always the sweetest. He was always my number one.

"Stay with me," he asks, and I look at him while he pushes my hair over my shoulder. "Stay with me today, tonight, tomorrow." He sits up now and kisses my bare shoulder. My arm wraps around his neck, and my fingers go into his hair. "I need you to come with me tomorrow."

"Where?" I ask, and he just smiles. "It's a surprise."

"Okay." It comes out breathlessly, and I hold his face in my hands now, his eyes red from the tears.

"I love you." His hands come to hold my face. "I've loved you my whole life."

"Jacob," I whisper his name.

"Every single part of you is ingrained in my brain. It's a part of my soul. Everything that you are is in me. Every single piece of my heart belongs to you," he says.

"You're my everything," I say as he leans down and kisses my lips once. I smile. "You've always been my everything." I kiss him now, slipping my tongue into his mouth just a touch.

"For eight years, I've dreamed of kissing you." His thumb comes out, and he traces my jaw. "Eight years of you in my dreams. This almost feels surreal," I say, looking down at his chest. My finger traces the outline of the cross that he now has on there. "It's always you." I look back up at him, and he grabs the back of my head now. My hair fisted in his hand, he crushes his lips on mine.

My mouth's already open for him as he slides his tongue into my mouth, and we both swallow each other's moans. My hand moves up his chest to his hair, and I crush my chest against his, wanting to get closer and closer to him. "I want to take you to my bed," he tells me when he lets go of my lips and slips his mouth over to my jaw and then roams toward my ear.

"Yes," I say while my heart beats frantically against my chest. He gets up in one swift movement, and with one hand around my waist, I lock my legs around his waist.

"You're really here?" he asks as he carries me past the kitchen toward the garage where we came in two days ago. He turns, and I want to look around at his house. I want him to take me room by room and tell me everything I've missed. "I'll give you a tour of the house after," he whispers as if he can read my mind. I look around his room, which is filled with just a big king-size bed and two side tables. He puts his knee down on the bed and slowly lays me down. He moves my hair away from my face. "I can watch you all day long and not get tired of it."

My hand comes up, and I palm his cheek in my hand. "For eight years, I chased you in my dreams only to wake up before I could get to you," I say softly, my thumb rubbing his face. "I didn't know why, and no matter how much I forced myself to dream again, I just couldn't get to you."

"I'm right here, baby," he says softly. "I'm always right here."

"We lost eight years because of me." I say something that I

143

finally realized when he poured out his heart to me. "If only I had stopped and listened to you. If only I had even for a minute thought there is no way." A tear escapes from my eye.

"Shh," he says. "For eight years, I blocked out the love I had for you because it was too painful. My chest would feel like it was being crushed. But the minute I saw you again, it's like it was yesterday. Everything was in front of me. Everything was right there. You were right there."

"There hasn't been anyone," I say. "No one but you." He opens his mouth, and he looks at me.

"You were my first," he tells me, and I know we were both each other's first, "and you are my only." He lowers his head to mine, and the kiss takes over, our tongues finding each other. The kiss starts slow, and then suddenly, our hands roam. I won't even deny that I start roaming first. My hands go from his shoulders to his back and then up again. His stomach dips in when I use my nails up his abs. He turns us on our side, and his hand goes to my hip, and then his hands move frantically up my shirt. He cups my breast in his hand, and I throw my head back. I finally cup his cock, and he's ready for me. "Fuck." He hisses when I move my hand up and down his covered cock. "Baby." He says my name, and I push him on his back at the same time as he sits up and takes my shirt off. "God, it's so much better than my dreams."

"I feel like I'm dreaming," I say, "and I'm afraid I'm going to wake."

He grabs my face. "It's real, baby."

I bend my head now and kiss his tattoo. "Show me it's real."

He rolls us over, putting me on my back, and hovers over me. His lips come down, and my mouth opens for him. He kisses me, moving slowly across my cheek and then under my chin toward my neck. I arch my back and watch his every move. I make a mental note of him. His eyes get darker when he pulls down one of my bra straps. He kisses the top of my breast and slowly pulls it down, and he takes one of my nipples into his mouth. My eyes want to watch him, but they close as his tongue twirls around one nipple and then the other. "Jacob." I whisper his name, my eyes feeling heavier than ever.

He moves his kisses lower on my stomach, and he stops, putting his hands on my stomach. My eyes open, and I look at him. "The next time, I'll be there from the beginning," he whispers, and his eyes look into mine. "One of these days, we'll have another baby." I don't say anything. I can't say anything past the lump in my throat.

My hand moves to his head, and I run it through his damp hair. "Make love to me." He gives me one more kiss before he slips off my shorts and panties at the same time.

"Fuck," he says, looking down at me. "Just a taste," he says and buries his face into my pussy. His hands open my lips so he can suck my clit into his mouth, making my legs open for him.

One thing we always did was experiment with each other. Neither of us was shy about what we wanted. I loved his mouth on me, and I always have. He uses one of his fingers to enter me slowly, and I almost squeeze his head with my knees. "Jacob." I can only pant his name. As he moves his fingers in and out, he never once lets go of my clit. He sucks it, nibbles it, flicks it, and just like that, the next thing I moan out is his name as I come apart on his tongue and his fingers.

I watch him take one last lick before he kneels in the middle of my open legs. He pulls down his shorts, and his cock springs out. I lick my lips, thinking of having him in my mouth. "Not now," he says to me and then he opens his mouth.

"What?" I ask, and he rubs his hands over his face.

"I don't have condoms," he groans, and I try not to laugh by rolling my lips.

"I'm on the pill," I say, "and I'm clean." He looks at me. "And, well, the last person I was with was you."

"Day before prom was the last time I had sex," he tells me, and I sit up. "If you put your mouth on my cock, this is going to be the fastest ending we've ever had."

I kiss his thigh. "The first time was thirty seconds." I look up, and he pushes me down.

He holds his cock in his hand as he crawls forward. "This might be faster." He rubs his cock up and down. My eyes fixate on his cock as he slowly slips it into me. I don't know why I expect it to hurt, maybe it's 'cause for the last eight years, I haven't had sex. He slips in, filling me, and we both moan. My legs wrap around his hips as he leans forward, and his hand goes beside my head. I turn to the side and kiss the inside of his wrist where his heart is beating, feeling his pulse under my lips.

"I love you," I whisper, and he kisses my neck before pulling out and thrusting in again. "Jacob." I call out his name when I wrap my arms around his neck. Our lips hover over each other, and he kisses me between thrusts.

I want him all over me. I can't seem to get close enough to him. "I'm almost there." His thrusts get harder now, my hips meeting his thrusts but getting pounded into the mattress. "Get there with me," he pants, and I take one of my hands and move it over my clit. "That's it," he says, and just like that, I'm running to the edge with him.

146

Twenty-One

JACOB

"Baby," I mumble when she sinks down on me. We just had pizza on the couch, and I reached over for her just to kiss her, and suddenly, I was ripping my shirt off her, and she was sinking down on me.

She looks at me as she rises and falls on my cock. Sex with us was always good, but fuck if it isn't even better now. It's like we're on a different planet. We were never shy when it came to sex, never shy to try things or ask for things, and it's no different now. "I need you," she says breathlessly when one hand grabs her ass and the other comes up to cup her breast. Leaning forward, I bite her nipple right before I pull it into my mouth. She moans, and I know that she likes it, so I do it to the other nipple. She slams down on my cock and rotates her hips, rubbing her clit against me. Both hands now are on her ass, and all I can do is squeeze them while she rides me. We don't say anything as I watch her take what she wants.

"You're close," I say when I feel her pussy get tighter.

"Yes." She pants and puts her hands on my chest to give her leverage to move faster. She sinks down on it three times and then rotates to get friction on her clit.

"Take it," I say, and she rides me fast. Putting one thumb in my mouth, she then rubs her clit with it, and she leans back, giving me more space to play with her. "That's it, baby," I say, ignoring the fact that my balls are getting tight. I'm going to come before her if she keeps this up. I rub her clit side to side, and her pussy just squeezes the shit out of my cock. "Fuck, you have one minute," I say between my clenched teeth, "then I'm taking over."

"No," she moans, throwing her head back. "It's my turn."

My hand moves from her hip to her breast, and I play with her nipple, rolling it between my fingers while my hand rubs her clit faster and faster. She finally crashes down on me, and I feel her pulse over my cock, and I come with her. She collapses on my chest, and I just hug her to me. I could stay in this position for the rest of my life. She buries her face in my neck, and I kiss her forehead.

"I love you," I say, and from this time forward, I'm going to say it every chance I get to make up for all the chances I lost out on saying it.

"I'm sorry." Two more words I'll tell her every chance I get.

She looks up at me. "It's over." Kissing me under my chin, she says, "This right here, me in your arms, it's all I can think about." I get up with her still attached to me. "Where are we going?" she asks me as I walk back to my bedroom.

"I haven't shown you the shower," I say, and when we finally get out of the shower, there is no hot water left.

She puts on one of my T-shirts to sleep in. She never did like sleeping naked. Even after we had sex, she would always get up and put on a T-shirt and panties. "Come here," I say, pulling her to me in the middle of the bed when she finally slips under the covers. Her head goes into the crook of my neck, her arm goes around my waist, and our legs intertwine. I just breathe her in, and for the first time in eight years, I feel complete. I feel whole.

All through the night, we wake when we are not touching, which leads to me making love to her and then her falling asleep in my arms again. When I finally wake in the morning, I look over and see that the bed is empty, and I spring out of bed. *She didn't leave*, I tell myself while I slip on my boxers. She wouldn't just leave, and when I walk into the kitchen, I stop to see her standing there in the middle of my kitchen, wearing my shirt. She looks over at me, and a smile fills her face. "Good morning."

I stalk over to her, my heart beating so fast as I push away the thought that she was gone. I grab her face, and she just looks at me. "I woke up, and you weren't there," I say, trying to catch my breath. "I thought ..."

"I was making us coffee," she tells me, her hands going to my waist. "I wanted to bring you coffee in bed."

My lips crush hers, and I kiss her frantically as if it's our last kiss. I pull the shirt off her, the need to have her naked under me is the only thing I can think of. "Jacob." I pick her up, placing her on the kitchen table. She feels my need to touch her, and just like that, she gives it to me with no questions asked. When I collapse on top of her, she lets me lie here, playing with my hair. "Well, that is one way to say good morning," she says, making me laugh, and I kiss her in the middle of her chest.

"I'll go clean up and make you breakfast," I say, slipping out of her.

"That sounds like a plan," she says, getting off the table. "I'll disinfect the table." I look at her over my shoulder. "Your son eats at that table." I roll my lips. "And my ass was just on that table." She shakes her head, walking over to pick up the T-shirt that I threw.

"You keep bending over in front of me, you'll be disinfecting the whole house." She cocks her head. "Especially that wall." I point at the empty wall where I'm going to take her against when we come home.

"Promises, promises, McIntyre." She winks at me and walks to my bedroom.

"Fuck," I say silently to myself.

"What?" Her head pops around the corner. I look at her. "What happened?"

"I'm happy," I say. "This is what it must feel like to be happy." Shaking my head, I say, "I have an appointment at ten."

"Oh, I can be out of here in twenty." She smiles at me, and I just look at her, and she stops. "What now?"

"You're coming with me," I say, walking to her. She waits for me, and we walk to my bedroom together.

"Well, where are we going?" she asks. Going to the bathroom, she takes off the shirt and starts the shower at the same time I take off my boxers.

"It's a surprise," I say and step into the shower. I leave the glass door open for her to step in, and she stands there, leaning on one of the sinks. "Are you not coming in?"

"If I come in there," she says, pointing at the shower, "it's going to lead to things."

I try not to laugh. "What kind of things?"

"Well, for one, I'm going to get on my knees," she says, and my cock stirs. "Then I'm going to sit you on that little bench." She points at the bench against the wall. "And I'm going to want to ride you."

"I see nothing wrong with anything that you just said." I turn to face her, and her eyes roam up and down my body.

"But then I won't get breakfast." She folds her arms over her chest.

"I have a compromise. We get breakfast to go, and everyone wins," I say, holding out my hands.

"Fine," she says, stepping into the shower as if I twisted her arm, "but we have to make this quick. I still have to clean the table."

I laugh at her, and she gets on her knees, taking me all the way back into her throat. It doesn't go as fast as she wants, and when I get out after her, she's already dried off with her hair wrapped in a towel. "I need coffee," she says, walking out of the room. When I finally get dressed and walk into the kitchen, she has two coffee cups on the counter, and she is wiping down the kitchen table with a bottle of Lysol.

"You ready?" I ask her and walk to the table in the living room, grabbing the piece of paper that I need.

"I have my mother's truck," she says, opening the cupboards in the kitchen and looking for a thermos.

"We can drop it off now or later," I say, walking to her and kissing her. "I love you."

"I love you, too," she says softly. Putting a hand on my stomach, she leans up again, and this time, it's her who kisses me softly.

"Let's go, baby," I say, and we walk out with her at my side. She is wearing the same thing she wore yesterday. "You need to bring over your stuff."

"What stuff?" she asks, walking to the passenger side of the truck, and I press the button to unlock the doors.

I get in at the same time as she does, putting my coffee in the center console, and buckling up. "Your clothes and stuff."

"What clothes?" she asks as I make my way out of my driveway.

"All of your clothes," I say.

"What?" She looks over at me, her mouth hanging open. "Jacob," she says, "I can't just move in with you."

"Why not?" I look over at her.

"Well, your son, for one," she tells me. "I haven't even met him, and all of a sudden he is going to come home and I'm there."

She's right. I know she's right, but I just got her back. The last thing I want to do is be without her. "So if I introduce you to Ethan, and we have a couple of dinners ...?"

"Then I will go home after the dinners, and I will come over and stay when he's not there," she says. "It's a big step."

I pull up to the shop and turn to look at her. "This is to be tabled for later." Leaning over, I kiss her lips. "Let's go." Turning to get out of the truck, I meet her on the sidewalk, and we walk up the tiled entryway and stop at the front door.

"What is this place?" Kallie asks, looking around, and the front door opens.

"Donnie," I say to the man who stands six foot eight with a beard down to his chest.

"Hey," he says, reaching out his hand to shake mine, his bulging arms fully covered in tattoos. "Come on in." He steps away from the door, and I put my hand on Kallie's back and usher her inside.

"Thank you so much for squeezing me in." I say once we are inside. "Donnie, this is Kallie."

"Pleased to meet you." He nods at her. "You ready to do this?"

"Yes," I say. He turns and walks to the closed door on the right-hand side. He opens both doors, and I look over at Kallie, who doesn't say anything.

We walk into the room that has a chair in the middle and shelves on the back wall with all different colors of paint. Donnie puts on his glasses and sits down on his stool and slides over to me. "Let me see what you have."

I take the white paper out of my back pocket and hand it to him. "What are you doing?" Kallie asks me when she sees me hand him Gabriel's footprint.

"Sit down. I'll start in a second," Donnie says. I pull off my shirt and hand it to her.

I sit in the chair, and she looks at me, holding my shirt close to her chest. "Okay, let's get this started," Donnie says, rolling to the side to get his ink gun. "What date do I have to add to the cross?"

"November thirteenth," I say, the birth certificate memorized.

"Oh my God," Kallie whispers, and I look over at her as she stands there with tears in her eyes.

"You can have a seat over there." Donnie points at another chair in the corner. She walks over to the chair and brings it to my side.

"Is this okay?" she asks, and he nods his head at her and smiles.

"We'll get the date added on here," Donnie says, cleaning my pec, "and then we'll add the footprint right under it." He gets up and walks over to the paper. "I'll be right back."

"Sounds good," I say, and he walks out of the room.

"You are adding Gabriel to your cross?" she asks, wringing my shirt in her hands.

"He's my son," I say and reach out to grab her hand. "He belongs on me."

"And his footprint?" She now loses the battle of her tears.

"It's the closest that I will ever get to him," I say and bring her hand to my lips and kiss her.

Twenty-Two

KALLIE

I sit on the chair right next to him, holding his shirt in my hand as he gets the footprint of our son tattooed right under his birthday that was added to his cross. When the doors first opened, I had no idea what this place was, and when I saw the chair, I still didn't know. But then everything clicked into place.

He sits in the chair, not even flinching when the needles go into his skin. Donnie does a little line and then wipes it off, repeating it over and over again, and I can't wait to see the final product. "I want one also." My mouth moves before I can even comprehend what I'm saying. Donnie looks up at me, and Jacob turns his head to look at me.

"On my wrist," I tell them, "right over my heartbeat."

"We can do that as soon as I'm done with his," Donnie says, and I just smile at him.

I sit now waiting in the chair for my turn, anxious and excited. When Donnie wheels away from Jacob, and says, "All done," but before I can see, Jacob jumps out of the chair and walks over to the mirror he has on the facing wall. I get up and walk over to him as I look at the little footprint he has now on his chest.

"It's so beautiful," I say, looking at it and wanting to reach out and rub my fingers over it after I kiss it. Instead, I look up at Jacob. "I love you."

"Okay, let's get that covered," Donnie says. "And, you," he says to me, "can get into the chair." I hand Jacob his shirt, and he goes over to Donnie, who covers it with a white bandage. "Take it off after four hours."

"Will do," Jacob says and puts his shirt on while Donnie comes over to me, and I turn my wrist for him.

"What color do you want?" he asks, and I look at Jacob.

"I want it to match Jacob's," I say, and he nods his head and goes to do something and then comes back with the tattoo gun in his hand.

"So is this your first one?" he asks, and I nod.

"Virgin skin." He jokes with me, and I laugh anxiously. "Everyone is different," he starts, "the pain could be through the roof or it could be nothing."

"Okay," I say and look over at Jacob who sits in the same chair I just sat in and holds my hand in his and kisses my fingers.

"It's going to burn," Donnie says, rubbing my wrist with his latex-covered hand. "Here we go." I wince when the needle goes through my skin.

"Oh my God." I say at the burning, but then it slowly goes down a notch. "Okay, this isn't bad," I say, and my eyes never move from his gun as he writes the date November thirteenth.

"There we go," he says, wiping it for the last time. I hold it up, and it's beautiful. He comes back over, getting it ready to be bandaged up. He wraps the white bandage around my wrist three times. "I'll give you instructions for care," he tells me, and I get up.

"You ready?" Jacob asks, and I nod, wearing a smile on my

face so big my cheeks hurt. We say goodbye to Donnie who tells Jacob he'll send him the bill.

Jacob's hand goes into mine as we walk back to the truck. He opens my door, but before I climb in, he pushes me against it. His hands go to my face, and he tilts my head up, kissing me. My arms go around his neck as he kisses me senseless in the middle of the sidewalk. "I love you."

"I love you more," he says, and then his thumb rubs my cheek when his phone rings in his pocket. He takes it out and looks at me. "It's Casey."

I look at him with worry as he answers, "Yeah." He looks at me and smirks. "She's with me. She's fine." He then hands me the phone. "It's for you."

I shake my head and grab the phone. "Hey."

"Hey, yourself," Casey says. "We are having lunch in twenty, and Mom wants you here."

"Well, then," I say, looking at Jacob, "set two more places."

"No kissy faces at the table." He tries to sound mad, but the snicker that comes out after ruins it. "We'll talk when you get here." In his true Casey self, he hangs up without saying goodbye.

"Well, then," I say, handing the phone back to Jacob, "we are having lunch at my parents' house."

"Good," he says. "About time we had the talk."

"Wait." My heart starts to speed up. "What talk?"

"Well, we need to tell them about Gabriel," he says, "and then we need to tell them that we're getting married." He tries to walk away from me, and I grab his arm to stop him.

"We're getting married?" I ask. My head is spinning, and just like the old Jacob, he walks back to me and grabs my face, knowing it calms me.

"I'd marry you today if you would have me," he says softly. "So yeah, we're getting married."

"Jacob McIntyre," I use his full name, "this better not be my proposal."

He throws his head back and laughs. "On one knee," I say, and he kisses me, "with roses." He shakes his head and walks around the truck. "Candles."

"Anything else?" He looks over the hood at me.

"Champagne," I say, getting in the truck. He gets in after I close my door.

"Small wedding or big?" he asks, looking over at me.

"Small," I say. I don't tell him that I planned the wedding when I was sixteen. It would have been the talk of the town, but now just him there with our closest family members and friends would be perfect. Thinking about it, just the two of us would be perfect.

"Outside or inside?"

"Outside." A picture of marrying him right under our tree by the creek flashes through my mind.

"Good to know," he says as we turn into my parents' driveway. He turns the car off and looks over at me. "You ready for this?"

"No," I say, shaking my head. "Not even close."

"Whatever happens, I'm going to be right there by your side," he says, and I look up at the house and see my mother coming out with a worried look on her face.

"Well, here we go," I say to him and open the door, stepping out. "Hey, Mom." I put up my hand to wave to her while I wait for Jacob. "Let's do this." I put my hand in his, and he brings it up and kisses it, making my heart flutter.

"Hi, you two," my mother says to us, and I see the smile on her face but also the tears in her eyes. We walk up the steps together, and she hugs me first. "Are you okay?' she whispers in my ear. I nod at her, and then she goes to hug Jacob. "It's good to see you again."

"Thank you," he says and then shocks us both when he

grabs her hand with his. "Thank you for being there for Kallie and Gabriel." He puts his arms around my shoulder as my mother wipes away tears. "He was in the best hands." She pats his hand in hers. The door opens, and my father comes out and sees that my mother and I are crying.

"What in the world?" he says, then looks at Jacob. "This is a surprise."

Jacob just nods at him. "Let's go inside. I don't think I can hold off Casey any longer," he says, laughing. "You ready, boy?"

"Bring it." Jacob looks at my father as he turns and walks inside, and we follow my parents.

I look up at him when we walk into the family room and see Olivia sitting on the couch with her feet curled under her with a glass of wine in her hand. "Ohhh, this is going to be good." She smiles at me and winks, then looks over at Casey. "You need to simmer down, cowboy."

"Darlin'," he says softly to her, and she raises her eyebrows at him.

"Okay," I start, "we might as well get this out of the way before lunch." I walk over to the couch and sit next to Olivia, who hands me the wine glass. I look over at her and smile. "I might need something stronger after this." I look at her with tears in my eyes.

I feel the couch beside me shift and look over to see Jacob sitting beside me. "Dad." I look at him. "You should sit."

"No," he says, shaking his head, the worry written all over his face as he takes off his cowboy hat and holds it in his hand.

"Billy," my mother says softly, going to him with tears running down her face, "you should sit."

"Is she sick?" he asks my mother, his eyes now filling with tears. "Are you sick?" He looks at me and asks me while I look at Casey, who looks like he's going to jump out of his skin.

"I'm not sick," I start and take a deep breath. "Here it goes," I mumble.

Casey barks out, "What in the hell happened to your hand?" He looks at the bandage around my wrist.

"I got a tattoo," I tell them. My mother's mouth falls open, and she sits down on the couch next to my father.

"You got a tattoo?" Casey asks me, shocked. "A tattoo."

"It's for life." Olivia leans to whisper in my ear. "Forever." She raises her eyebrows.

"I know." I smile back at her. "It's the date of my son's birthday," I say out loud, and then I look around the room. My father sits there in shock, his cowboy hat falling to the floor. My mother puts her hand in front of her mouth, and Casey folds his hands over his chest, his jaw tight.

"What are you talking about?" Olivia looks at me and grabs my hand in hers. My other hand slips into Jacob's.

"I was pregnant when I left here," I say. "I just didn't know until I was two months along."

My father now with tears pouring down his face. "Why didn't you say anything?"

"I was going to, but every single time I tried, I got scared." I tell the truth. "There was just so much going on."

"Where is the baby?" Casey's tone is tight, and I look down and then at Jacob, who brings me to his chest.

"Sadly, my water broke at twenty-one weeks, and he didn't make it." I look over at my father who groans, and my mother gets up and goes over to him. I get up and walk to my purse by the door. Grabbing my wallet, I walk over to them and take out the picture of me and Gabriel. "This is Gabriel." I hand my mother the picture, and she holds it for my father, who sobs with his hand over his mouth.

Casey walks over and looks at the picture, and he turns and looks at Jacob. "All alone," he hisses. "She did that shit all by herself."

"Cowboy." Olivia gets up and walks to him, grabbing his hand in hers. He looks at her, and something she says settles him, and he just looks at me.

"That's not fair," I say. "I didn't tell him. I told no one. I couldn't ..." I wipe away the tears. "He was my secret, and he was my everything."

"Kallie," Olivia says softly, and Casey now puts his arm around her. "I'm so, so sorry that you had to keep this to yourself."

I blink away the tears. "It was hard not to tell everyone how beautiful he was." I smile. "But now I get to share him with you all." I turn to look at Jacob. "We can share him with you now."

"I love you," he says, burying his face in my neck, and I feel his tears on my neck.

"I'm a grandfather," my father says, looking at my mother, who cries her own tears and wipes his away. "You should have told me."

"I know," she says softly, "but it wasn't my story to tell."

"I want to put his picture up on the wall," my mother says. "I want his picture on the wall where he belongs with our family."

"Right after lunch, we can go into town and get frames." My father pulls her to him.

"Well," I say, "this was a bit easier than I thought it would be."

"We haven't told my mother yet," Jacob mumbles, and I look at him. "Might as well get it over with."

"There is no way she is going to Cristine's house without me," my mother practically yells. I look over at her and so does Jacob.

"Charlotte," my father says, and my mother shakes her head.

"No." I look at her, and she looks back at me. "You aren't going to her house. If you want, invite her here."

"What am I missing?" Jacob says, and I look back at my mother, wondering the same thing.

"Nothing." My mother tries to pretend that there is nothing, but now Casey speaks up.

"If we are sharing everything, might as well share that, Mom." He looks at her, and I know he knows. When I look at my father, even he avoids my eyes.

"What is going on?" I ask them, angry.

My mother just looks at Jacob. "I'm sorry," she says. "When you left, your mother came over here." She sits down, and all eyes are on her. "She was angry that you were suffering and blamed it all on Kallie." My leg starts to tremble while she continues the story. "Everything was her fault." My mother points at me. "Well, I told her that we should let you two work out your own things. She said some not nice things, and I'm not repeating them, but—"

I hear a roar come out of Jacob at the same time I look at my mother. "Tell me."

"No," she says, shaking her head.

"I want to know," I say, and my stomach is already in my throat.

"Kallie," my mother says softly, "it doesn't matter now."

I stand and drop Jacob's hand from mine. "It matters to me."

My mother looks at Jacob almost for permission, and he just nods at her. "I want you to know that her words were nothing but her being angry."

"Mom." I say her name too loud.

"That Jacob obviously didn't love you or he would have never strayed." My mother says the words, and although I thought I was ready for it, it cuts me right through the heart.

"That if you kept your house in order, this would never have happened."

"That fucking—" Casey says. Olivia's hand snaps out, and she blocks his mouth.

"Excuse me," I say, looking at the floor, the tears making it difficult to see. "I need to ..." Walking toward the stairs, I run up them and barely make it to the bathroom before a foot is shoved in right before I can close the door.

"Oh, no, you don't," Jacob says. I don't say anything because his arms go around me, and I sob in his arms. "She is never going to talk to you like that ever." I can't say anything. "I swear, Kallie, she won't."

Pushing off from him, I leave him standing there, looking at me, as I close the door. "She isn't the only one who is going to think that or has thought it," I say, wiping the tears from my face, "and I know I shouldn't care, and I know it isn't the truth."

"It's not the truth." He comes to me. "I've loved you my whole life. I've loved you when I didn't know what love was. I wish I could make it all go away. But ..."

I raise my head. "I know, and I would never let you put Ethan in that position or take you away from him."

"Now with regard to my mother, she will never ever say those words again. I promise you that," he takes me in his arms. "I agree with your mother. I'm going to tell her to come here. No way will you walk."

"No," I say loudly, "she will not make me walk with my head down."

He smiles. "Okay, but I want her to come here. I want her to be the one walking with her head down."

"Okay, fine," I say softly. "I didn't think of it like that, but yeah."

There is a knock on the door, and we both look over as the door creaks open. "Hey," Olivia says softly, "so no pressure or anything, but Casey is foaming at the mouth, and I think he said something about fixin' to and a hill of beans, and I swear I have no idea what he's saying."

Laughing now, I look over at her. "It doesn't amount to a hill of beans?"

"Yes." She points at me. "That's the hill of beans."

"It means it doesn't amount to anything and is hog wash."

"That's what your father said," Olivia now says, and I hear my mother calling my name.

"If I don't get some food on the table," she starts to say, "they are both going to get madder than a wet hen."

Olivia looks at me. "Beans, hog wash, and now a wet hen." She shakes her head. "It's like I'm on another planet."

"Tell my mother we'll be right there." I look at Olivia, who nods and closes the door.

I walk to the sink and wash my face off and then dab it with the towel. "You ready?" Jacob asks, and I look at him. "Let's get some food in you."

We walk downstairs and into the kitchen where my mother looks like she spent the night and morning cooking. "I'm so hungry." I sit in the chair and look over at my father, who just smiles at me, and then look over at Casey, who side-eyes Olivia. "What's with him?"

"Nothing," Olivia mumbles, looking over at him. "Let's eat."

Twenty-Three

JACOB

"What time will she be here?" Charlotte asks from behind me, and I look up. I've been sitting outside since I called my mother, trying to calm down. I've been trying not to lose my shit, to be honest. When I heard what my mother said, I wanted to jump into the truck and go to her house and yell at the top of my lungs.

"She should be here soon," I say. She smiles at me and walks back into the house, and the door opens again.

"Hey," Kallie says softly, and I look over at her and smile. Fuck, she makes me so complete. She makes me want to have it all and do it all. "You okay?" She puts her head on my shoulder and wraps her arm around mine.

"You need to calm down."

"I am calm," I lie, and she just looks at me. "Okay, fine, I'm raging." She gives me time to talk. "There is so much." I shake my head. "I'm not holding back this time."

"Jacob." When she whispers my name and leans in to kiss me, we hear the crunch of rocks, and both of us share a look. "Let's get ready to rumble." She jokes with me, and I look over at my mother as she gets out of her car. She looks at us, and you see the frown on her face right away.

"Well," she says when she gets close to us, "what is this all about?"

"Hi, Mom." Standing, I wait for Kallie to get up, and I slip my hand into hers.

"Hi, Cristine," Kallie says, and my mother just nods at her. "We should get out of this heat."

I wait for her to walk into the house, and I look at my mother, but she avoids my eyes, which makes me even angrier. I wait for her to walk in before me, and I hear shouting right away.

"You can't use biscuit in that sentence." I hear Casey say followed by Olivia shouting at him.

"Why not?" We walk into them facing off at each other. "If you are not nice, you get no biscuit." I hear Kallie burst out laughing, but Olivia doesn't stop as she walks to Casey with her finger out, pointing at his chest. "You can say hens get wet and beans in a frill, but I can't use biscuit?"

"Okay, you two," Charlotte says. "Take this to your house." She looks at Casey and then looks at Olivia. "Tomorrow, we can go over the list of food that you can use and what you can't use."

"Let's go, cowboy," Olivia says and walks by him. I'm expecting him to make her walk by him, but he stops her by grabbing her hand.

"There is so much I need to say right now," Billy says, and I just look at him sitting at the table.

"Well, then ..." Charlotte claps her hands. "Would you like some tea?" she asks my mother, but Mom just shakes her head.

"What was all the fuss to get here?" my mother asks, and then she looks at Kallie, who is now holding my hand. "One week in and I see that things are back to normal." She looks at me. "God knows how long it's going to last this time," she mumbles, and I'm about to snap at her, but Kallie starts first.

"The reason we called you here is to tell you firsthand about something." She looks at me. "There are things that happened when I left and—"

"You mean when you gave up on my son and hightailed it out of town without looking back?" my mother asks.

"Okay, then," Charlotte says, and Billy gets up with her tone and she looks over at him, "I've held my tongue for eight years." She comes to stand next to Kallie, and she holds her hand. "You were my best friend," she starts to say, "and when I needed you by my side, all you did was blame Kallie. You never once looked at the whole picture."

"That's because your daughter was to blame for all of this!" my mother shouts.

"My daughter carried your grandson by herself!" Charlotte yells out this time, and my mother just looks at her. "That's right, Cristine, while you went around town telling everyone how happy you were that you were going to have a grandson, I had to hold my daughter's hand while she buried *our* grandson. She did that all by herself. Carried the pain and the burden by herself. A piece of her gone forever." I look over at Charlotte.

"Now I'm sorry that I'm doing this without easing into it, but I've had enough of you blaming Kallie for this." My mother puts her hands to her chest, and Charlotte walks over to the picture that Kallie took out before. "This is Gabriel." She hands my mother a picture, and she takes it in her shaking hand. "He was born November thirteenth." She looks over at Kallie who now wipes her own tear away. "And he was beautiful."

"He looks like Jacob," Mom says and wipes her tear away.

"Mom, this stops today," I finally say. "This blaming Kallie stops today." I hold onto Kallie as I pour it out for her. "I made a mistake, one mistake, and I've paid for it. I've watched you mourn Dad. I've stood by you when Travis hightailed it after Dad died. I've stepped into his shoes, and not once have I complained about it. Not once did I ask you for anything." I take a deep breath. "I'm not asking you. I'm telling you this stops today." I look over at Kallie, who just stares at me. "If you can't respect Kallie, then it's over. I won't call you, and I won't come over. You'll lose another son. Just this time, I'm going to be right in front of your face with my happiness. Mine and Kallie's because she's my choice, she's always been my choice, and she will always be my choice. I will always choose her."

"Jacob ..." my mother starts, and I hold up my hand.

"There are no second chances, Mom, but I was lucky enough to get one, and I'm going to do what I need to do to keep her. I want to make her happy, and I want her to be comfortable to walk anywhere without people pointing and throwing the mistake that I made in her face." I look at Kallie. "I made a mistake with Savannah, and I broke the trust she had in me. I can't even begin to think how it would feel for it to happen to me. And if I'm honest"—I shake my head—"I don't think I could survive it."

"Jacob." She says my name and picks up our joined hands and kisses my fingers.

"I want a life with her, and I want to have all the kids she will allow me to have with her. I want to wake up with her and go to bed with her. I want to sit out on my porch when we're eighty and watch our grandkids run around. I want you in that life also, Mom, but I won't compromise Kallie to make you happy."

"You have a son," my mother says. "You see your child in pain, and you would do whatever you need to do to make him happy. That is what I was trying to do."

"The things you said about Kallie were horrible," Charlotte says. She shakes her head. "Never once did I say anything about Jacob. Not one time did I throw anything in your face. I can forgive, but I'm not going to forget. I just can't."

"Mom." Kallie wraps an arm around her.

"No," she says. "For eight years, you were gone. We didn't have you for Christmas, we didn't have you for birthdays, we had nothing. I had to sit down on Christmas Day and have an empty chair, and I couldn't do or say anything to anyone. I'm not going to do that anymore. I will not let her chase you away."

"I won't," my mother whispers. "I won't. I'm so sorry, Kallie." She looks down now. "But you didn't just run from Jacob, you ran from me, too. You were like a daughter to me, and you just cut me out." She wipes tears from her eyes. "I lost a daughter that day also, and I know I should have reached out, and I should have done so many things differently, and for that I'm sorry." She looks at Charlotte. "To both of you."

"Thank you," Kallie says. "I wish I could go back eight years, and things would be different, but we all made choices that day, and we all have to live with them."

"Well, this has been exhausting," Billy finally says and walks over to the liquor cabinet and takes out his bottle of whiskey. Pouring himself a shot, he drinks it and then pours another. He walks over and takes out more shot glasses and fills them and lifts one. "To Gabriel."

We all walk over to the table and grab one. I raise my glass. "To my boy Gabriel," I say and grab Kallie and kiss her. "To our boy."

Kallie and I sit on the swing outside on her porch, and I look in at my mother and Charlotte talking quietly on the couch as she holds the picture of Gabriel in her hand. "Are you going to go pack a bag?"

"When is Ethan coming back?" she asks.

"Savannah texted me today that she's staying until Tuesday since Ethan has a ped day on Monday and Tuesday," I say, and she looks at me.

"Don't you work tomorrow?"

"I do," I say. "And?"

"Well, I guess I could come and then come here when you leave," she says, and I just look out at the trees.

"Or you could stay at my house." I look over at her, and she just looks at me.

"I have to work, and all my stuff is here," she says, "so I will come over tonight, but tomorrow, I'll come here and work. Then you can pick me up after work, and I can come back to your place."

I nod my head. "That sounds good. Tuesday night, I want you to meet Ethan."

"He's just been away from you for four days, and you're going to just bring me in?" She turns to look at me.

"Yup," I say. "I already spoke to him about you. So laying the groundwork has already started."

"Jacob." She says my name, and I stand and look down at her.

"Kallie, I'm done wasting fucking time," I say. "I'm done. Starting tomorrow, I don't care who knows and who doesn't that we are together. Actually, starting now, I don't care. We can go down to Main Street and make out in the middle of the street and give them all something to talk about."

She rolls her lips, hiding the smile. "So touchy."

"Yeah. I am. Now go get a bag," I say and then shake my head. "Fuck it, don't get a bag. You can wear my shirt to bed." I pull her up by her hand, and I'm about to put her over my shoulder when she pulls her hand away.

"Hold your horses. I'm going to pack a bag." She shakes her head. "Don't be blowin' up a storm." I smile now.

"There's my country girl." I walk to her. "Pretty as a peach."

"Hush your mouth and kiss me," she says, the same thing she used to always say to me when she had enough of what we were talking about.

Twenty-Four

KALLIE

"I'll pick you up at five," Jacob says from beside me, my eyes looking out the window. "Kallie." He calls my name, and I look over at him. "What's wrong?"

"Nothing," I say. Looking back out the window, I don't want to make eye contact with him because he's going to see right through me. "I'm not feeling well."

"Really?" he says like he doesn't believe me, and I wouldn't either. This morning, I was fine. I woke up with him giving me little kisses on my bare shoulder, my tank top pushed up while he held my breast in his hand. It took a matter of sixty seconds for him to turn me on my back and slide into me. For the past two days, it's been bliss to wake up with each other every single morning and have dinner with each other. And then just sitting with each other before bed is everything, but, and there was a huge but. "You were fine this morning."

"Yeah." I watch the trees fly by as he drives me home. "Well, it just hit me."

"Interesting," he says, and I hate the way he says it as

171

though he knows I'm bullshitting. I know I'm bullshitting, but I don't need him to know.

"Does this not feeling good have anything to do with you meeting Ethan tonight?"

I glare over at him. "No."

"Liar," he says, trying not to laugh, and looking at the road while he grabs my hand and brings it to his lips. "It's going to be fine."

"Is it?" I ask him. "I don't know if this is a good idea." He side-eyes me. "Maybe we should just go slow. Like maybe this weekend I can come over for breakfast, and we can see how that goes." He pulls into the driveway of Casey's house. "Or we can have cake or something."

"Baby," he says, and I hate his tone. Okay, fine, I love when he calls me baby because his tone is soft and filled with love. "I'm not going that long without you."

"Well, I'm not going to be sleeping at your house with Ethan there. That is just ..." I don't say anything because he pulls me to him. "Jacob."

"Kallie, you sleep with me," he says, and I want to push away from him. "We just won't tell him."

"So, you want me to sneak into your house?" I ask, shaking my head.

"For now, that is what we have to do," he says, kissing me.

"No, we can be grown-ups about this and have dinner, and then I can see you tomorrow morning."

"Fuck no," he says. "Now kiss me because I have to go to work."

"Fine, we can table this discussion." I barely get the words out before his mouth is on mine, and I'm lost in his touch, in his kiss, lost in him. "Be safe."

"Always." He kisses me one last time, and I open the door, turning to get out. He grabs my hand one last time. "He's going to love you."

"Or hate me for taking you away from him," I mumble and get out of the car, and he rolls down the window.

"I love you, Kallie," he says, and I look over my shoulder. "I'll call you later."

I turn and walk up the steps toward the front door, ringing it first. I made the mistake of walking in yesterday and found them dry humping each other on the island. "It's open!" Olivia yells, and I stick my head in. "It's all clear. Cowboy is not home."

"Good," I say, stepping into the entrance and walking to the kitchen where Olivia has set up her office on said island.

"The coffee is fresh." She smiles at me, and points at the coffeepot on the counter that looks brand new.

"Thank you," I say. Putting my bag down, I take my laptop out and start it up, then walk to the coffeemaker. "Why does it smell like bacon?"

"I made Casey breakfast this morning," Olivia says, and I look over at her for two reasons. One, my brother has never made a meal in his life. In fact, my mother still cooks all his meals. And two, Olivia doesn't cook. "I know, I know ..." She puts up her hands. "But I wanted to do something nice for him."

"I mean, we had to throw out five pots because you burned them so bad."

"Okay, fine." She smiles at me, and I look over at her. She doesn't have one ounce of makeup on her face. Her hair is piled on top of her head. She has a nice glow to her face from being out in the sun in the afternoon. She is also wearing a white tank top with black yoga pants and a long sweater over her. "I asked your mom for instructions." I look at her, and she just stares at me. "Don't think too much into it, please."

I shake my head. "Honestly, I've never seen you happier," I say. "You aren't even wearing makeup."

"I know." She smiles. "And my skin is so soft. I think it's the water," Olivia says.

"I'm going to give my notice," I say, putting the cup of coffee to my lips.

Her mouth flies open. "I mean, are you sure?" She puts her own cup down and leans forward. "This is a big change. You're going from city to country."

I smile. "I've always been country." Tilting my head, I say, "And I've always been in love with Jacob." She looks down. "It was one mistake, and I have forgiven him for it."

"At the end of the day, he is your person," she says. "He makes you happy."

"For my whole life, I knew that I would be his wife," I say. "For my whole life, nothing made me happier than seeing him. Then I lost him, and I lost myself. I was me, but there were all these pieces of me missing and now ..." I smile. "Now with him, seeing him, touching him. He was my missing piece."

She puts her hands to her chest. "Bless your heart." I shake my head, laughing. "Did I not say it in the right way again?"

"I have no idea," I say, "but you're learning."

"So you are really going to leave and come live here?" she asks, and I nod. "What are you going to do?"

"I have no idea, and I'm scared as fuck, but the other way is me being away from him, and I'm not okay with that option."

"Does he know?"

"He doesn't. I think he's afraid to ask." I walk to the chair next to her and take out my phone. "I'm going to call Meryl right now." I take the phone and dial Meryl, who answers right away.

"Hey," she says, answering the phone with us on speaker. "I just got your email and Olivia's. You guys are on fire." She laughs. "I should send you two away more often if you are going to come back with all these ideas."

"Yeah," I say, thinking of the whole look we did yesterday. We incorporated some country flair to the chic pictures they sent over. I was a graphic designer, and Olivia was a stylist, and the two of us together made quite the team. It also helped that we understood what the other was saying. "I'm calling with some news."

"Oh," she says, picking up the phone now, "is everything okay?"

"Well, we are still laying low. The detective is supposed to call us by the end of the week with the result from the finger-prints found at the scene," I inform her. When we called her in the middle of the night, she knew it wasn't good, and she knew from the news stories that it was going to get a lot worse before it got better, so she was more than okay with us leaving.

"Well, that's good to hear," she says. "So what's up?"

"I guess there is no easy way to say this." I think about when I started at the magazine five years ago, and how she took a chance on a brand-new student straight out of college with no experience. I think about my life back in LA and how different it is to the country. I used to do spin class five days a week, and I used to have celery juice every single morning. Now I have coffee and lard, and I couldn't be happier. "I'm staying here."

"What do you mean staying there?" she asks.

"I mean, when this is all over, I'm only going back to LA to pack up my stuff, and then I'm moving back." Olivia reaches over and hugs me, putting her head on my shoulder.

"I see," Meryl says.

"I love my job, I really do, but I love my life here even more. And now that I'm back, I can't think about leaving."

"What if I said you can do both?" Meryl says right away, and I look at Olivia, who looks at me with her eyes wide.

"I would say what do you mean?" And then Olivia chimes in.

"Actually, she would say hush your mouth." She looks at me and whispers, "That was good, right?" and I nod, smiling.

"Oh, Jesus, do not tell me that you are turning country," Meryl says, and Olivia laughs out loud.

"Heavens to bitsy, no!" Olivia shrieks, and I laugh.

"It's heavens to Betsy," I say, and she just shrugs.

"Anyway, as I was saying, what if you worked from home and then flew in a couple of times a year? You can skype from wherever you are during meetings," she says, and I clap my hands quietly. "That way I'm not losing my favorite graphic goddess, and you still do what you love."

"Oh my gosh," I say, overjoyed.

"I reckon she's happy," Olivia says, and we all laugh now.

"I'll send you a new contract, and you can look it over," Meryl says, "and, Olivia, don't go falling in love with any cowboys."

"The saying is save a horse and ride a cowboy." She winks at me, and my face goes into a grimace.

"Gross," I whisper, and she just shrugs. I see a little mark on the top of her breast when her shirt dips low. "That's even grosser." I point at the mark, and she pulls up her shirt.

"He's your brother. Apparently, branding me turns him on," she says, and I fake vomit.

"I will keep an eye out for your email," I tell Meryl and hang up the phone. "Holy shit."

"That's amazing. We are still going to work together," Olivia says. "Just not live with each other." She pouts. "I'm going to have to get a new roommate." She puts her hand up and her thumb down. I push away from the island and walk over to the fridge.

"We should have a piece of pie to celebrate." I pull out the homemade cherry cake that my mother made yesterday. "Do you want a piece?" I ask, and she shakes her head.

"I'm full as a tick." She puts her hand on her stomach, and

I just look at her. "It's not my fault, it's Casey's. He walks around all the time with all these sayings."

"You know I love you," I say, "but I just want to make sure that neither of you get hurt." She looks at me.

"We both know this is temporary," she says. "We're just having fun."

"Okay, but ..." I start to say, and she puts up her hand to stop me.

"As soon as everything dies down and it's safe for me to go home, I'm leaving," Olivia says, and I don't discuss it anymore since she changes the subject with work.

We work side by side for the next five hours, only stopping to use the bathroom and drink, and when my phone rings, I pick it up without looking at the name. "Hey, baby." His voice comes out soft. "Whatcha doing?"

"Working." I stop what I'm doing to answer him, the smile on my face is automatic when he's around or talking to me.

"I'm done for the day, and I was going to swing by and get you," he says, and I'm about to make an excuse when the doorbell rings. "Answer the door."

I walk to the door, and when I open it, he's standing there with a bouquet of wildflowers. "For you." He hands them to me, and my hand drops from my ear with the phone in it. He comes in and kisses me right away, crushing the flowers between us. "Missed you," he says when he finally lets me go. "You ready?"

"She is," Olivia says, and I look behind me, and she stands there with her feet crossed, watching us with a huge smile on her face. "Have fun." She hands me my bag.

"What time are you getting Ethan?" I ask, and he looks at me, opening the truck door.

"As soon as you get in the truck." He smiles and ushers me into the truck, and before I know what is going on, he pulls up to his house. "Savannah will be here in ten minutes."

I look over at him. "I hope you don't mind, but I don't want to be there when she is around. I get that we all have to live in this situation, but I'm still ..." I shake my head. "I understand if you want to bring me back home, and I can come when he is already here."

"You can wait in the kitchen," he says. "She never comes in." I look over at him. "Even though we are co-parenting a child together, it's still my place." He looks down and then over at me. "It was just something that we never crossed. I don't go into her place, and she doesn't come into mine."

"Do you want to go into her house?" I ask.

"Nope." He gets out of the truck and so do I.

"I'm going to ask Casey to pick me up at nine," I say when he unlocks the door.

"Kallie." He says my name. "Let's get through dinner," he says.

"What are we eating?" I ask, and he shrugs while I shake my head. "I'll see what I can come up with." I'm about to walk away from him when he grabs my hand and pulls me to him.

"You haven't kissed me," he says softly, pushing my hair away from my face. "I missed you."

"I missed you more," I say, putting my hands around his waist, and my stomach flips and flops like a fish out of water. He tilts his head and leans in to kiss me, and when I think it'll be a soft kiss, it's needy with his tongue slipping into my mouth and his hands buried in my hair. I arch my back into him at the same time a car pulls up, and I hear a car door close. I look over and see Savannah getting out of her car with Ethan, and they just look at us. "Oh my God," I say, and then I look at him.

"I'll wait for you inside," I say, and he just nods. "Also I might be throwing up in case you are looking for me."

I walk into the house and close the door behind me. Walking into the kitchen, I open the fridge and spot a couple of things, and when I slam the fridge door, I come face-to-face with Ethan, and he's alone. "Um, hi," I say to him as he looks at me with eyes just like his mother.

"Hi," he says, putting his bag on the couch and coming over.

"Where is your dad?" I ask, suddenly nervous and anxious and scared of this little boy.

"He's outside with Mom," he says, getting on the stool. "They are having an adult talk." I look toward the door, not sure what to do.

"Um," I stutter, "it's nice to meet you." He smiles at me.

"What's for dinner?" he asks, not even giving a shit that I was just almost dry humping his dad while he sucked my face.

"I was going to do mac and cheese," I say, and he nods at me.

"Cool," he says, getting up. "I'm going to put my things away." Grabbing his bag, he starts to walk, and then he stops. "You really are pretty," he says and heads to his room.

"Thanks," I whisper and let out the huge breath I was holding in.

Twenty-Five

JACOB

"Go inside, buddy," Savannah says to Ethan. "Give me some sugar." She smiles at him. He hugs her around her waist, and she bends down to kiss him. "Love you."

He skips and hops over to me, coming up the steps. "Hey, Dad," he says, and I lean down and kiss him on the head.

"Hey, kiddo. Did you have fun?" I ask him, and he nods. "Go inside and say hi to Kallie."

"Okay," he says and walks into the house and closes the door behind him. My heart speeds up, knowing that Kallie is going to have a bit of a panic attack when he comes in without me.

"What's up?" I ask her, my eyes watching the door the whole time.

"So what's the story with Kallie?" she asks. "I know that you guys are together, but I thought maybe you would talk to me before introducing her to Ethan." My head turns back to Savannah the minute she says the last word.

"Excuse me?" I try not to lose my shit with her. I haven't told Kallie that the reason that I don't have her in my house is because the only thing I want from her is Ethan. I don't tell

180

her that after she left, I was never alone with Savannah in one room. I would bring Beau or meet her in the open so people would see that we weren't together.

"It's the first girl you introduce him to, and there is a lot of history there. I was just thinking that you would discuss it with me. This is a big thing in his life, and I don't want him to feel like his life is being uprooted with it."

I walk down the steps to her, and I want to shake her. "Savannah, the only thing I talk to you about ever is Ethan," I say, and she looks up at me. "We made a pact eight years ago, and I've kept up my part in it. But things are different now. Kallie is back, and a part of my life, and if I have anything to do with it, she'll be an even bigger part of it."

"Trust me, Jacob, I know too well the pact that we made," she says softly. "I just don't want Ethan to feel like—"

"She's here, and she's back," I say. "I'm going to talk to Ethan tonight about it. He's a good kid, and he'll adapt. And if he doesn't, we'll make sure that we are united in this, and that no matter who I'm with or who you're with, he knows we are still his parents."

"Fine," she says and walks away from me to the truck. "Text me later to tell me how it went."

"Sure thing," I say and turn to walk into the house. I walk to the kitchen and see Kallie putting a pot on the stove. She looks over at me and glares. "I'm sorry."

"He came in here," she whispers, looking over my shoulder to make sure the coast is clear, "and I didn't know what to say."

"Well, where is he now?" I look around, and she points to his room.

"Unpacking his bag," she tells me and wipes a tear away. I walk to her and take her in my arms. "He's beautiful," she says. "So beautiful."

"He is," I say, and I kiss her lips.

"Why were you outside?" she asks, and I know I should tell her.

"Nothing." I lie to her, and she glares at me.

"If we are doing this, no more secrets." She pushes away from me, but I hold her tighter.

"Okay, fine, she was just surprised that I was introducing you to Ethan so fast," I say.

"And?" she prompts.

"And I told her in no uncertain words that it was none of her business and that I was going—" I don't finish because she puts her hand on my mouth when she sees Ethan come into the room.

"I have math homework," Ethan says, "but I need help."

"You go help him. I'm going to get dinner going," she says, and I kiss her.

"Get your things and we can do it at the table." I look at Ethan and walk to the table. I help Ethan with his homework while pots bang in the kitchen, and I hear her hissing on the phone with someone when she looks at me. "You don't have bread crumbs."

"Okay." I don't know if she's asking me or telling me.

"I'm making mac and cheese, and, well, it's not really mac and cheese without the bread crumbs." She throws up her hands. "I'm going to need your keys."

"For?" I ask and look at Ethan, who is pretending not to laugh at Kallie freaking out.

"For?" she says. "Did you not just hear what I said? I need bread crumbs."

I shake my head, and I want to tell her that it's going to be fine without it, but I'm not going to add fuel to that fire. "My keys are in the truck."

"Okay, I'll be back." She turns off the stove. "Ethan." She looks at him. "What's your favorite dessert?"

"Um," Ethan looks at me and then looks at Kallie, "apple crumble pie."

"Okay," she says, "I'll see what I can do." She turns and walks out of the house, slamming the door behind her.

"Um, Dad," Ethan says, "is she going to bake me a pie?"

"Kiddo." I look at him. "I have no idea."

"She's jumpy," he says to me, and I look at him.

"She's nervous," I say. "She was nervous to meet you."

"Why?" he asks. I tap my fingers on the table.

"Well, she knows how important you are to me," I say.

"And she wants me to like her." He nods at me as though he's solved the puzzle.

"Yeah, kiddo." I lean over and kiss his head. "She wants you to like her."

"She's pretty," he says.

"She is," I agree with him. "She's always been." I grab my wallet and take out a picture that I've kept hidden in the back. It's frayed at the edges and the color has changed from glossy to a yellow tint. "This was us." I show him the picture we took on prom night. The only one I had on my phone.

"You were so small." Ethan jokes with me. "You got guns, Dad."

"Who taught you that?" Laughing, I take the picture back from him and put it back in my wallet, right behind the picture of Gabriel.

"Uncle Beau," he says, and I shake my head.

"Anyway, kiddo, if you can do me a favor and give her a chance, you'll see how awesome she really is," I say softly, and I'm about to say something else when the door opens and slams closed, and she comes rushing in with a glass plate in her hand.

"Okay, I got the bread crumbs," she huffs. Going to the stove, she turns it on. "And the only thing my mom had was apple pie, but she's going to make you apple crumble pie tomorrow so we can have it then." She looks at Ethan. "Or you can have it all yourself," she says and points at the apple pie in front of her.

"Your mom made apple pie?" Ethan asks.

"She has this huge freezer where she puts all her baked stuff in, and she told me that all I had to do is put this in the oven for an hour, and it'll be perfect." She looks like she is flustered, and I get up and walk over to her.

"Baby," I say, and she just looks at me like she is going to cry.

"I'm ruining it," she whispers. "I'm ruining everything."

I hold her face in my hands and wipe away the tears that come down her cheeks. I can see she was crying before she got into the house. "Baby, nothing is ruined," I say. "Will you come and sit down with us so my boy can meet you, please?"

"But I have to make dinner for him," she says. "He's a growing boy, Jacob." She looks down. "The way to a man's heart is through his stomach."

"I love you," I say, kissing her.

"Jacob, you just kissed me, and Ethan is here," she says.

"He needs to get used to it," I say. The timer goes off, so I let my hands fall from her face.

She turns and goes to put the pasta in the water, and I go back to the table to help Ethan, who just smiles at me. "She is going to make me pie tomorrow," he says.

"Yeah, kiddo, she will," I say, and she makes us mac and cheese. She tops it with bread crumbs and bakes it at the same time as the pie.

"I forgot vegetables," she says, putting her hand to her head.

"Good," Ethan says, and I shake my head when the oven buzzes.

"Go wash up, please," Kallie says to me, and Ethan pushes away from the table, putting away his homework and walking into the little bathroom on the side to wash his hands. "Can you get me three plates, please?" she asks, and I walk over and grab three plates for her. I look at the baked mac and cheese and lean in to kiss her neck.

She scoops out three plates and leaves it to sit for a second to cool off while she sets the table. "Where does everyone sit?" She looks at me, not wanting to sit in Ethan's or my place and it be awkward.

I'm about to tell her that she can sit anywhere when Ethan pipes in. "I sit here." He points at the chair where he was just sitting in to do his homework. "And Dad sits there." His hand moves to the head of the table. "And Grandma sits here." He points at the chair next to him. "You can sit in front of me and next to Dad."

She looks at him with a smile. "That sounds like a good plan."

He gets in his chair, and Kallie puts his plate down in front of him and another plate down where I'm going to sit. I wait for her to get her own plate and come to the table. She sits down and looks at me. "Do we say grace?"

Again, Ethan pipes up. "I can say grace," he says, and we join hands. "Bless this food that Kallie made and bless the apple pie."

I try not to laugh, and we all say, "Amen."

Dinner goes smoothly even though Kallie barely eats anything. She just pushes things around on her plate, and I look at her when Ethan asks for a second serving. She's about to get up when I put my hand on hers. "I'll get it. You eat." I point at her, and she smiles tightly.

Ethan tells her all about football and the positions he plays, and he tells her about his favorite subject in school, which is gym, and how he hates math. When he finishes eating his two plates, he brings his plate over to the sink and puts it on the counter. "Can we have pie now?"

"How about you go take a shower and let the pie cool?" I say, and he starts to frown.

"I think it'll be better cooler," Kallie says, getting up. "This way, the ice cream won't melt when I put the scoop on it."

His eyes go big. "Ice cream and pie?"

Kallie throws up her hands. "Well, yeah, silly, how else do you eat apple pie?"

"Not like that," he says and looks at me. "Why haven't I had it like that?"

"I have no idea," I say and then look at Kallie, who is putting the dishes in the dishwasher, "but go shower, and we can have it."

He hops and skips to his bathroom, and I count, "Five, four, three, two, one," and point when he says my name.

"Dad, come turn on the water." I get up and walk over to Kallie first.

"Coming!" I yell down the hall. "You didn't eat," I tell Kallie, and she just shrugs.

"I thought I was going to throw up I was so nervous." She looks at me, and I see the tears in her eyes. "He's perfect."

"Yeah," I admit. "It's why I know what I did was wrong, but why I can't regret it. If I regret it, I regret him, and I can't do that." No matter how much I wanted to hate Savannah for doing what she did, I couldn't hate her because of Ethan. It was a very tight line, and no matter how many times I wanted to hate her, I couldn't do that to Ethan.

"You're a good man," she says. "I may sometimes want to kill you, but a good man none the same."

I'm about to lean in and kiss her when Ethan yells my name again. "I'm naked, and things are shrinking, Dad!"

She rolls her lips. "I'm going to clean up." She kisses my lips. "You make sure things don't shrink."

"I love you, Kallie," I say, and she looks me in the eyes.

"I love you, too, Jacob." She says the words quietly and then leans in to kiss me one more time before I go off and make sure my son is okay.

Twenty-Six

KALLIE

"I'm not staying," I hiss at Jacob when he takes my purse, my phone, and my shoes away from me. "What if Ethan wakes up?"

"Then he will call my name," he says.

We just had the best dinner ever. Sure, I had a mini freak-out and rushed to my mother's house and had a panic attack on her couch while I made her get me bread crumbs and a fucking apple pie. I didn't know if she had it or not. If she didn't, she would just have had to make one and deliver it to me because there was no way I would have let Ethan not have apple pie.

I didn't eat much since the nerves in my stomach were all over the place. I kept holding my breath and waiting for him to tell me he hates me and that no one is going to love his dad. But none of that happened; it was the opposite. He sat there with a huge smile on his face the whole time, while he ate two huge plates of my mac and cheese. And then when he took a shower and came out in his pjs, I wanted to hug him and smell his hair. Instead, I blinked away the tears, watching Jacob be a dad. I always knew he would be a great father, but seeing it is so much more.

We ate apple pie, which is now Ethan's favorite, and he asked if he could bring a piece to school tomorrow, so I already cut and packed it for his lunch. I sat listening to Ethan rehearse his nighttime story, and just when I thought my heart couldn't get fuller than it was before, it almost explodes.

Jacob comes to the couch after turning off the lights, and he lies down and takes me with him. After kissing and him holding me and me almost falling asleep, I got up and got ready to go, except he was hijacking all my stuff.

"Jacob, please," I beg, and he grabs my hand, turning and walking to the kitchen where he turns off all the lights except for the light on the stove and then walks to his bedroom. "I don't think this is a good idea."

"I think we are thinking too much, and we should get into bed." He tosses my things down on the bench in front of the bed. "How is this? I will set the alarm for six thirty." I fold my arms over my chest. "Okay, fine, six because I want to get some loving before Ethan gets up at seven."

"Oh, no way, mister," I say, shaking my head. "It's one thing for me to sleep here but something else entirely for us to have sex here with your son five feet away from us." I point at the door. "This is not even an option."

"Let's play it by ear." He winks at me, and I just roll my eyes. "Do you want to shower first, or should we?"

"I'm not even going to give you an answer to that question," I say, and he goes to the bag and takes all my stuff with him. "What are you doing?"

"I'm not leaving your stuff out in the open where you can run." He laughs. "Just be happy I'm not cuffing you to the bed." The door closes behind him, and I sit on the bed to wait for him to get out of the shower. He walks out with a towel around his waist and shirtless, and I don't even think I can stick by my no sex with Ethan in the house. "Your turn," he says, and I get up, but he stops me and kisses me. My hand goes to his tattoo of Gabriel's footprint. I lean forward and kiss the scab. "Love you, Kallie," he says, and I just nod at him, then go to the shower.

When I finally finish in the bathroom, I'm expecting to find him in bed waiting for me, but what I find is him in bed snoring softly. I walk to the bed and turn off the light, sliding in with him. He must feel me get into the bed because his hands reach out and pull me to him. "Night, baby," he mumbles, and even though I want to hold out, I follow him into sleep.

It's crazy how easy we get into a routine of waking up at six with a soft alarm, and even though I held out the first day with no sex, it's a losing battle the next day when he wakes me with his mouth between my legs. I cover my mouth when I come on his face, and when he flips me over and slides into me from behind, I bury my face into the pillow. By the time the seven o'clock alarm rings for Ethan, we are showered and sitting at the island while I drink coffee, and he reads his emails. I help Jacob prepare lunch for Ethan and clean up, getting into the car at the same time. I make dinner for us while he does homework with Ethan.

"Kallie." Ethan calls my name while I'm frying chicken steak.

"Yeah, buddy?" I look over at him.

"Will you be at my game tomorrow?" he asks. I know he has a game because it's all he was talking about.

"Of course she's going to be there," Jacob says from beside me now.

"Cool. Maybe we can all go for ice cream after," he says and looks down at his homework.

"Um," Jacob says from beside me, and I shake my head, not wanting Ethan to sense anything.

Dinner is normal, but my nerves are setting in. When I get up to clean up in the middle of dinner, Jacob looks up at me and continues to eat, and luckily, Ethan doesn't sense anything.

After dinner, it's the same routine except I don't wait on the couch for him. Instead, I take a shower, and when I get out, he's waiting for me on the bed. "What's the matter?"

"Is Ethan asleep?" I ask, and he nods. "I'm not sure how I fit in with all this." I say the truth. "I know how I fit in here." I use my finger in a circle. "I know where I fit in this"—I point at him and me—"but out there, I don't know how I fit in."

"Kallie," he says, not coming to me, "there is nothing to doubt when it comes to me and you. In here or out there. I want you beside me every single day, for every single event." He walks to me now. "I never want you to doubt us ever. Never again." He grabs my face, and I put my hands on his.

"People are already talking," I say. "My mother has been fielding calls and when she went out the other day, she got stopped and—"

"And after tomorrow, it'll be old news," he whispers. "You know how it goes, Kallie. In two days, something else will be the talk of the town."

"I guess," I say, looking down. I give him a fake smile, and he knows it.

The next day when he drops me off, I walk into the house, and even Olivia knows something is off. "I have to run an errand," I say, looking at my watch and seeing that it's a little after two.

"Going anywhere I should know about?" She wiggles her eyebrows at me. "Afternoon quickie."

I shake my head. "No," I say, grabbing my purse, and I walk out of the house before she asks me anything else, and I walk into my parents' house.

"Mom!" I yell, and she comes out from the kitchen,

wiping her hands on a towel. "I'm going to borrow the truck, okay?"

"Sure, honey, is everything okay?" she asks, looking at me, and my stomach already feels like I'm going to vomit.

"Yeah, I just have to pick a couple of things up. I'll be back soon." I grab her keys and pull out of the driveway before anyone else can stop me. I drive with the radio off, and my thumbs strumming the steering wheel.

When I pull into the parking lot, I notice it's empty except for one car. I walk to the door and pull it open. It's different in the daytime. No loud music, no lights blaring. Just a quiet country bar. "Sorry, we're closed," Savannah says and turns around to see me standing here.

"I won't be long," I say and walk in just a touch. "Are you here alone?"

She looks at me and nods her head, coming around the bar, and I see her in just plain jeans and a tank top. This woman who destroyed my life, destroyed Jacob's life. "What can I do for you?" she says with just a touch of attitude, and I'm so fucking over it.

"Well, I'm happy that you know I'm not here for idle chitchat," I say.

"What are you here for?" she asks.

"I'm here for one reason and only one. Ethan," I start to tell her and just like the mama bear that I know she is, and exactly like the mama bear I would be at the mention of her son's name makes her stand up straight. "I'm not going to beat around the bush. We are never going to be friends. I don't really want to even be here right now, but it's not just about us anymore, is it?" She starts to say something, but I hold up my hand. "I'm not going away like I did eight years ago. I'm here, and I'm staying. I think for Ethan's sake we should be cordial in front of each other when we are together for him," I say and now she laughs out.

"How would you know what is the right thing to do?" she says, and I look at her.

"Well, for one, the right thing would have been to actually be honest." I give her a cheap shot, and I have zero fucks about it. "You knew he would protect you," I say. "You knew he would never tell you no. You knew that it would destroy us, yet you didn't care. You just did what you wanted to do for you."

"I did what I had to do for my child," she hisses. "You wouldn't know anything about that."

"That's where you're wrong," I say. "You see, while you were parading around this town pretending to be pregnant with his child, I was actually pregnant with his child," I hiss, and now it's her turn to stand there with her mouth hanging open and shock all over her face. "Pregnant and alone, thinking that the love of my life and father of my child lied to me, but it was all a lie. I gave birth to my child alone, and I buried my child alone because of you. And I won't ever fucking forgive you for that."

"Kallie," she says with tears in her eyes, "I would never."

"I don't want your sympathy. I don't want anything from you. Now or ever. I've spent this past week with Ethan, and I've fallen in love with him." I force myself not to let the tears that are burning to fall. "And for him and for Jacob, I will pretend that we get along."

"Kallie," she says again, this time not even pretending that she is crying. "I never wanted to hurt you. I never wanted to hurt Jacob. He is my best friend, and I don't know where I would be without him." I don't interrupt her. "I'm sorry, so sorry."

"Sorry will not change anything," I say, and I know nothing either of us can say will make anything better. Nothing she will say will bring back Gabriel. Nothing will ever make anything okay. "I'll see you tonight," I say and turn to walk out of the bar. The door slams shut, and when I get to the truck, I stop and rest my forehead against it.

I get in the truck and make my second stop of the day. I pull up and park behind his truck and walk up the steps, opening the door. There is no one sitting at the front desk, and then Grady comes out from the back. "Well, look at this," he says, looking at me, and I just smile at him.

"Hi, is Jacob here?" I ask, and he nods.

"Follow me," he says, and I follow him back to Jacob's office.

He looks up from his desk and smiles when he sees me, getting up. "Hey there." Walking to me, he kisses me. "What are you doing here?"

"I'll be at my desk," Grady says and closes the door behind him.

"Are you okay?' Jacob asks, and I look down.

"I went to see Savannah," I say, and he picks up my hand and kisses it, "I'm sorry I didn't tell you before I went. I just."

"Baby," he says softly.

"I just wanted her to know that I'm not going anywhere and that no matter how I feel about her"—I let out a big breath—"that Ethan will never feel it from me."

"You're amazing," he tells me, and right before he kisses me, a siren goes off.

Grady shouts, "Shots fired at Casey's house!"

Epilogue One

JACOB

Five months later

"Are you sure this is a good idea?" Ethan asks from beside me as he watches me climb the ladder against the tree.

"Yeah," I huff out, holding on to the ladder that tethers left and right, making me hold my breath while it wobbles.

"If you fall and break something, Kallie is going to freak out, Dad," Ethan says. I don't need him to tell me that this is crazy right now. I also don't need him to tell me that if I do break something, Kallie will do more than freak out.

"You are not helping, Ethan," I say between clenched teeth as I throw the light over one branch, letting it fall over swinging. Ethan walks to it to stop it and keep it in place.

"That's one," he says, "only a million more to go."

"Not a million," I mumble, "just two more dozen." I climb up another step and toss another cord, and he stops it also. When I had this idea, it played out a lot better in my head. *How hard could it be*, I thought to myself, and now that I'm five minutes in, I should have gone with rose petals in the middle of the living room.

Except I didn't wait all this time to propose to her and have it be mediocre. No, my girl deserves the best. I just hope I can do it in one piece. I move the ladder over slowly, ever so fucking slowly. When I finally step back down on the ground and walk over to the switch, I look over at Ethan. "Do they not work?" he asks.

"I don't know. Let me flip the switch," I say, and when I do, the lights illuminate. The light bulbs hanging on their power cord hang from the branches of the trees.

"It's cool, Dad," he says, and I look at it.

"It is, but it's not done," I say and grab the white sheet of lace I have and place it over two branches and let it hang. "Just a few more touches."

"I'm going to go sit on the rock," he says, grabbing my phone and going over to sit on the rock that I brought here all those years ago for Kallie. The same rock that not so long ago she wanted off her property. The same rock where I told her I loved her for the first time. I place the other two pieces of lace around the tree with the seven white lanterns on them. I take the battery-operated candles from the bag and turn on the switch on the bottom, and the tips light up.

"Okay, kiddo," I say, looking over my shoulder at him. "How does it look?"

"She'll like it," he says. It's been over six months, and Kallie has made our home a home. She is on top of everything that has to do with Ethan, she has taken him into her heart, and it's just flourished. He didn't just get Kallie. He got Charlotte and Billy, who treat him as if he's theirs, and I guess in a little way he is a part of all of us.

"Okay, let's get home before she suspects something," I say and walk back to the truck.

"She's going to know right away," Ethan says. "She smells trouble, and she also smells when you're fibbing." I look over at him and know that he's tried to get one over on her many times, but she has a way of knowing.

"She does," I say and wait for him to get into the truck before I get in and start the truck. "You are going to behave for Gammy Charlotte and Gramps Billy, right?" I ask, and he just nods.

"Gramps Billy said he's going to take me fishing," he says with a huge smile on his face. With all this shit around us, my boy finally got himself a grandfather who would die for him without batting an eye. If it's the weekend, you know that Ethan is going to be with Billy any day he can. The two are thicker than thieves.

"Did he?" I ask him as I pull up to the house and see that Charlotte is sitting on one of the rocking chairs she put outside with Billy next to her. The both of them are smiling when they see my truck. Billy is the first one to get up and walk down the two steps toward the truck.

Ethan opens the door as soon as I put it in park and turn off the engine. "Gramps," he calls him, "I'm here."

"That you are, my boy," he says, leaning down and kissing him on the head. Charlotte is coming down now.

"Now, don't you give him all the love," she says, and Ethan walks over to her and hugs her around her waist and looks up at her. "I think you've gotten taller," she says, and he nods his head. "It's a good thing I just put the pie in the oven."

His eyes light up. "Is it apple?"

She looks at him. "Is there any other kind of pie?"

"Nope," he says, and she kisses him. I grab his bag and hand it to him. "Bye, Dad," he says to me and comes to give me a kiss before running back to Billy, who takes his hand and walks inside.

"Is everything set?" Charlotte asks, and I nod.

"I think so," I say, and she smiles at me, coming to kiss my cheek.

"It's a long time coming," she says, and I nod to her as she turns to walk into the house after Ethan.

When I walk into the house, I yell for Kallie right away. "I'm in the kitchen!" she yells, and I find her putting away the groceries. "Well, hello there." She smiles when she sees me, and I walk over to her and take her in my arms.

"Hello there," I say, and my lips find hers. Since the first day she came over, she hasn't left. I mean, she tried to, and well, she lost that battle.

"Did you drop off Ethan?" she asks, always wondering about him, just another reason to love her.

"I did," I say. "Your father is taking him fishing."

"Oh, he's going to love that," she says. "What did you want to do for dinner?"

"I was thinking that we can lay low." I push her hair away from her face and kiss her neck. "And then maybe just ..."

She looks at me, and her eyes squint as though she's not sure about something. "What are you up to?"

"Me?" I avoid her eyes. "Nothing."

"Jacob McIntyre." She calls me by my full name, and now I know she's going to get it out of me.

"Okay, fine," I say, turning and grabbing her hand and pulling her out the door.

"Wait," she says, trying to keep up with me. "You didn't lock the door."

"I'm the sheriff," I say over my shoulder. "No one will actually break into my house." I open the door and pick her up, putting her in it and grabbing the seat belt. "You are going to have to do me a favor and not ask me anything and just go with it."

"What in the heck?" she says, and I make her stop talking by kissing her.

"Please," I whisper, and she looks at me.

"Okay," she says softly, and I kiss her one more time before closing the door and getting in the truck. The whole way toward the creek, I go over my speech in my head. When I pull up to the clearing, she looks over at me, and I just shake my head. When I get out of the truck and walk around to her side, I grab her hand. My hand suddenly starts to get sweaty, my heart starts to speed up just a touch, and I'm suddenly so nervous, which is crazy since this is Kallie. It's me and Kallie; it's always been me and Kallie.

We walk hand in hand while the sun starts to set, and when we get to the rock, she looks up and sees everything I've prepared. "What in the ...?" The lights that I strung up on the trees hang at different lengths, and the lace hanging looks like a canopy. I look at her and look back at the lanterns around the tree illuminating the tree.

I walk her to the tree and turn to look at her, and all she does is look around while tears fall down her cheeks. "Jacob," she says to me when I get down on one knee.

"I had this whole thing prepared," I start to tell her. "I went over the speech for the last week. I even rehearsed it with Ethan."

"Oh my gosh." She laughs. "He didn't even tell me."

"Well, he knew how important it was." I smile. "Kallie, you don't know this, but I was going to propose to you on prom night." I say the last secret I have kept to myself. She rolls her lips together and tries not to sob. "I had this ring," I say, taking out the brown ring box that has been with me ever since I bought it, "inside my jacket pocket. I was going to bring you up here and ask you to be mine. To marry me and make me the luckiest man alive."

"I would have said yes," she says. "A hundred times, I would have said yes."

"Kallie Barnes, I fell in love with you when I was probably in diapers. I loved you even when I didn't know I did and having you beside me makes me the man I am. I want to have more babies with you," I say. "I want to fill the house with toys, and I want to watch your stomach grow with my baby. I want to hold your hand when you get scared. I want to kiss you when you go to sleep and when you get up. I want to wake up and see my ring on your finger every single day. I want to grow old with you and share all your tomorrows with you. I love you so much more than any words can say."

"Yes," she says, stopping me. "Yes, I'll marry you." She bends down, taking my face in her hands. "I've loved you forever. I will love you always."

Epilogue Two

KALLIE

Three years later

"I hear you." I put my hand on my ever-growing belly. Opening the fridge, I grab a piece of pie while my little one kicks me as if he's in kung fu training.

"Kallie." I hear Ethan call me, and he runs into the kitchen. "Gramps is here." I look over at him and smile. He's grown a foot in the last six months. He runs over to me, kissing my cheek, and he doesn't even have to get on his tippy toes to do it. He bends and kisses my belly, something that he started when I was pregnant with Amelia two years ago.

"Did you pack everything?" I ask, and he just nods and turns to run out of the house to my father who is waiting. I waddle to the front door and see my father hugging him and then looking up and smiling at me.

"Hey there," he says to me when I make it onto the porch. "Get in the truck, and I'll be right there." Ethan nods and turns to wave at me one last time. "How's my girl doing?"

"Which one?" I ask, laughing. "Amelia is living up to the terrible twos. I think she's aiming to be the best one at that.

201

This morning, she threw a tantrum when I told her that she was only allowed to have three crayons to color with instead of ten. She informed me very clearly that I was not the boss of all the crayons and that she would be telling Daddy on me." I shake my head. Amelia was a surprise, to say the least. With everything that happened with Olivia, I forgot to take my pills a couple of days, and four weeks later, I was told that I was with child. To say I was scared was the understatement of the year. I didn't even want to get up for fear that I would lose it.

I stayed in bed for the first three months, and I refused to even move until Jacob called in my mother and Cristine who sat with me and cried on my bed when I told them my fear. Slowly, I got up a little bit more every single day. Every single day, I would feel kicks, and I would pray that she would come, and at thirty-nine weeks and after fifteen hours of labor, she came screaming out into the world. And I mean, screaming. She was fit to be tied, and that should have been my first clue that she would be a handful. Holding her in my arms for the first time, I sobbed for what seemed like forever. With Jacob by my side and Amelia in my arms, I literally thought my heart would explode with happiness.

Amelia was everyone's pride and joy. And I mean, every-one. I don't think she was ever not in someone's arms. Plus, Ethan doted on her like she was glass, making sure everyone who was holding her took care of her. Hold her neck, she doesn't like to be lying down too much, she likes to look around. He was the best big brother there was.

"Well, when Amelia wakes up, why don't you call your mother and have her come get her? Give you a break," he suggests, and I smile.

"That sounds like a great idea," I say, and he gets in the car and pulls out of the driveway at the same time as Jacob pulls in. He waves at them and comes to a stop, getting out of his truck and coming to me. My heart still skips a beat when I see him. My stomach still gets little flutters when he smiles at me. "Hey there. You're back early."

"I got done earlier than I thought." He walks up the steps and kisses my belly, whispering to him. "Hello," he says when he takes the second step, and I kiss him. "How are my beautiful girls today?"

"Well, Amelia was not too pleased that you were not there to carry her to breakfast," I say. "She said she is going to have a talk with you."

He shakes his head. "Just like her mama," he jokes, and I roll my eyes.

"She also is going to discuss with you the rules for crayons. FYI, it's three at a time," I inform him, and I know that he's going to give in and give her more. She is the apple of his eye, and she has him wrapped around her little pinky. The minute her lower lip trembles, it's game over.

"Three," he says, and then we hear our daughter open the door and walk out.

"You left me," she says, rubbing the sleep out of her eyes. Her soft blond curls bounce as she carries her stuffed bunny in one hand. "I was scared."

I'm about to tell her that she's fine, but Jacob leans over and takes her in his arms. "We would never leave you." His gold band is on his hand. The minute we found out I was pregnant, we got married two weeks later. That was me putting my foot down. I wanted to have a wedding dress and flowers and all that jazz, so he gave me seven days. With all the contacts I've made over the year and with Olivia's help, I was ready in three.

We are about to walk inside when we hear another car pull up, and I look over to see it's my mother. She stops the car and gets out with a huge smile on her face. "There she is," my mother says, and Amelia smiles huge while she looks over at my mother.

"Hey there," Jacob says, and as soon as my mother gets close enough, Amelia leans forward to go into her arms.

"Oh, hello, my angel girl." She kisses Amelia who lays her head on my mother's shoulder. "I missed you."

"You saw her yesterday," I point out and shake my head while Jacob comes and stands next to me, putting his arm around me.

"Well, it was a long time ago." She side-eyes me with a glare and then whispers to Amelia, "Do you want to come over to the house, and we can bake cupcakes?" Amelia shoots up, and her eyes go big and the smile on her face is huge as she nods. "Then we can have a sleepover in the princess room." Another thing, my room at home is now the princess room.

"Yeah," she whispers and then leans in. "Can we do choco-late chip?"

"We can do anything you want." My mother holds her to her chest. "Say goodbye to Mama and Daddy."

"She doesn't have shoes on," I say, and she shrugs.

"I have three pairs at home," my mother says and then whispers in her ear. "Let's get going."

"Hey," I say, and they look over at me. "I want kisses." I walk down the step and to them, pushing Amelia's soft curls behind her ear. "Love you, baby girl." I kiss her lips.

"Honey bunch and oats." She finishes the sentence that I started saying to her when she was a year old.

I watch them drive off, waving and then look over at my husband. "What's that look about?" He stands there at the top of the step with his arms folded over his chest.

"It's what happy looks like," he says to me.

"It also looks like you want something." I walk to him.

"If it's from you, I want it all," he says, holding my hand and walking inside with me.

I walk over and grab a piece of pie, zapping it in the oven for a couple of minutes since my boy only likes warm pie. I eat the piece and then go sit on the couch next to Jacob, who moves over so I can lie on him a bit, and he places his hand on my stomach.

I lie here watching whatever he is watching, not even caring at this point. I don't care about anything when I'm in his arms. My eldest son is fishing with my father, my daughter is baking cupcakes, and my baby is kicking my husband's hand —I couldn't be more content. I never thought this would happen. I never thought I would be here after I lost Gabriel. My future was black, and I didn't see anything. I thought I would never have this. I turn my head to the side and kiss Jacob's arm. "Love you," he says to me, and I look up.

"Love you more," I say. "Thank you." He looks at me confused. "For giving me a second chance at life."

"Baby," he says, "thank you for giving me the world." He leans forward and kisses me.

Books by Natasha Madison

Southern Wedding Series
Mine To Have
Mine To Hold
Mine To Cherish
Mine To Love

The Only One Series
Only One Kiss
Only One Chance
Only One Night
Only One Touch
Only One Regret
Only One Moment
Only One Love
Only One Forever

Southern Series
Southern Chance
Southern Comfort
Southern Storm
Southern Sunrise
Southern Heart
Southern Heat
Southern Secrets
Southern Sunshine

This Is
This Is Crazy
This Is Wild
This Is Love
This Is Forever

Hollywood Royalty
Hollywood Playboy

Hollywood Princess
Hollywood Prince

Something Series
Something So Right
Something So Perfect
Something So Irresistible
Something So Unscripted
Something So BOX SET

Tempt Series
Tempt The Boss
Tempt The Playboy
Tempt The Hookup

Heaven & Hell Series
Hell and Back
Pieces of Heaven
Heaven & Hell Box Set

Love Series
Perfect Love Story
Unexpected Love Story
Broken Love Story

Mixed Up Love
Faux Pas

Printed in the USA
CPSIA information can be obtained
at www.ICGtesting.com
LVHW092249280324
775804LV00031B/656